Wonderland

A TALE OF HUSTLING HARD AND BREAKING EVEN

Nicole Treska

SIMON & SCHUSTER

NEW YORK LONDON TORONTO SYDNEY NEW DELHI

100 YEARS

SIMON &
SCHUSTER

1230 Avenue of the Americas
New York, NY 10020

First Simon & Schuster hardcover edition July 2024

SIMON & SCHUSTER and colophon are registered trademarks of
Simon & Schuster, LLC

Simon & Schuster: Celebrating 100 Years of Publishing in 2024

For information about special discounts for bulk purchases, please contact
Simon & Schuster Special Sales at 1-866-506-1949 or
business@simonandschuster.com.

The Simon & Schuster Speakers Bureau can bring authors to your live event. For
more information or to book an event, contact the Simon & Schuster Speakers
Bureau at 1-866-248-3049 or visit our website at www.simonspeakers.com.

Interior design by Carly Loman

Manufactured in the United States of America

1   3   5   7   9   10   8   6   4   2

Library of Congress Cataloging-in-Publication Data is available on file.

ISBN 978-1-6680-0504-0
ISBN 978-1-6680-0506-4 (ebook)

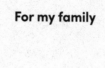

For my family

TELEMACHUS' DETACHMENT

When I was a child looking
at my parents' lives, you know
what I thought? I thought
heartbreaking. Now I think
heartbreaking, but also
insane. Also
very funny.

—*Louise Glück*

CONTENTS

PROLOGUE
MYSTIC CITY BY THE SEA

My grammy, Elsie Duca, on Wood Island, East Boston, 1947

How do you turn the province of drunks, sailors, and hookers into a dream of bright escape? You build Wonderland, one of America's first amusement parks, located on the water right outside of Boston. Wonderland only operated for a few bright seasons, from 1906 to 1910, but its legacy shines on.

Wonderland was built just off Revere Beach, a long, rough crescent of soft sand where over a century of Bostonians, including my entire family, escaped the broiling New England heat. Developers tried and failed to make a go of the Revere waterfront for years before the park was built. The beach was accessible, served by a narrow-gauge railroad, but it was also known for its criminal element. At the beginning of the twentieth century, amusement parks were built in resort towns and on boardwalks all over the East Coast, so Revere got another shot. Wonderland was built over a marsh bought cheap with rides and designs borrowed from the Chicago World's Fair, the St. Louis Expo, and Brooklyn's Dreamland Amusement Park, in Coney Island.

And while compound financial disasters would close Wonderland's gates after only five seasons, its opening day saw 100,000 residents arrive by railroad in their Sunday best. Working-class Bostonians from the West End strolled alongside Jamesian Back Bay elites.

The entrance on Walnut Avenue shone with 30,000 lights, under which patrons passed into the promenade. The electric lights at Wonderland were as big a sell as any of the attractions, and the park capitalized on their dazzle. The parades and entrances lit up the North Shore.

An elevated boardwalk circled a central canal where Shoot the Chutes, an early version of a log ride, sent thrilled patrons in skiffs skidding out across the water. Wonderland's Chutes were the biggest in the world, brought to Revere direct from the St. Louis Expo. The Scenic Railway followed the park's perimeter, carrying Bostonians far above the silted band between the firmament of East Boston and the Broad Sound.

Next to Shoot the Chutes, the infant incubator pavilion advertised LIVING INFANTS. Steel boxes sat in clean lines, and a pipe along the ceiling delivered oxygen to each incubator. The babies inside were visible behind glass doors and monitored by visitors and a full medical staff. Other amusement parks across the country featured infant incubators, as well. Premature babies weren't given great odds at survival, and Dr. Martin A. Couney wanted to show people that with warmth, protection, and clean air to breathe, these newborns could survive their circumstances. A safe space for babies was a radical new idea.

Many of the park's larger attractions were meant to reveal the far-off world to Bostonians and bring it closer. Shows like Pawnee Bill's Great Wild West, the Japanese Village, and the South before the War were enormous productions, built on lots that housed hundreds of performers and elaborate sets. They were also built on flagrant stereotypes and exploitation and were criticized even at the time. In between lots, there were sideshows, fun houses, pageants, and talent shows to stoke the wonder of anyone with five cents to spare.

SOME OF WONDERLAND'S RIDES AND attractions must have been cathartic to witness.

Fighting the Flames was a headline attraction where the facade of a town square burned every night. Guests packed an amphitheater and watched the drama unfold. The townspeople onstage swept sidewalks and bought vegetables. They were unaware of the curling smoke that the audience witnessed. The crowds celebrated as heroic off-duty firefighters arrived to extinguish the all-engulfing flames.

No one died when the square burned. No one was ruined. No one's business or home disappeared, just like that. It was a roaring good time, a simulated disaster, a controlled burn.

Bostonians knew fire and flames. Less than forty years before, the Great Boston Fire of 1872 rolled across the city, burning the most beautiful blocks you'd never see: the whole of the Financial District, the entire downtown. Sketches of the aftermath showed a city of rubble, ruins—something ancient and gone forever.

The Cyclone roller coaster, built along Revere Beach in 1925, burned down in 1969. My mom, my dad, my entire family, still talk about the roller coaster that existed for them but never for me.

Under the Sea joined Wonderland after the first season. It

5

featured an enormous tank where Houdini knockoffs broke free of their complicated bindings and swam for freedom and fresh air. Divers in heavy suits walked underwater, under enormous pressure. Women in mermaid suits looped the depths of the tank, their long hair haloed toward the surface. The newspapers called the performers "human fish."

In 1919, almost a decade after Wonderland closed, a fifty-foot tank of molasses exploded on Commercial Street in Boston's North End. A faulty, overfull tank with bad rivets burst on a warm January afternoon, and two million gallons of molasses flooded the streets in a thirty-five-mile-per-hour, fifteen-foot wave. Shrapnel from the tank tore through the steel beams of buildings. The heavy molasses, under pressure, flowed like water. Its viscous mass destroyed the neighborhood, killing some on impact and suffocating others in its dark amber. The North End smelled sweet for years.

Wonderland's Descent to Hell Gate spiraled riders through Dantean circles of hell in a boat before dropping them precipitously into the Underworld, where they met the devil on his throne before they could meet daylight again.

My family circled around and around, though daylight often eluded us. For instance, the *Boston Globe* detailed my father's arrest for federal drug trafficking in 1985. He walked into work at the post office and was tackled by federal agents in a sting operation. A real sticky situation. We saw him out on bail before he went to prison for two years. When he got out, I was seven and my younger sister, Lindsay, was four. She didn't remember him. My family met the devil regularly.

Finally, there was Love's Journey. The ride was advertised as "crazy, sentimental, and sensational." It promised a revolutionary experience that spun lovers in suspended rotation through the various stages of romance. There were children dressed as cherubs, heart-shaped carts, and a confusion of confetti dumped on rider's heads. This roving search felt familiar too. Aren't we all out searching for love?

THE CYCLONE'S RUINS CAME DOWN in 1974, five years after it burned and five years before I was born. The blizzard of '78 swept homes into the sea, up and down Revere Beach. The storm permanently shuttered storefronts and destroyed the seawall. After that, only seedy clubs and bars returned to the strip. The last vestiges of the Mystic City by the Sea were defeated by fire and ice.

During my childhood in the 1980s and 1990s, murders spiked. Swimming was banned because of water pollution, and a day at the beach represented a real dedication to the cause. Yet even then, there we were, slathered in sunscreen. Stay close to the wall, my mother would tell us. Watch out for needles. Don't get in too deep. Don't drown.

Don't drown. This was, and still is, the Boston model of progress. If you live under its lofty blueprint, get ready for a brutal sea change. Wonderland, Logan Airport, Government Center, Mass General, the Big Dig. Boston's rich history of greased handshakes and popping flashbulbs for the businessmen, politicians, and mobsters making deals created upheaval and impermanence for the rest of us. We were sold out and told it was for the public good. This constant turmoil of development came with great fanfare but often resulted in disappointment and agony for Bostonians.

Whole neighborhoods were razed, leaving large parts of the city stunned and punchy. Our homes—our grandparents' and parents' homes—were bulldozed, milled into interstates, hospitals, and sports arenas. Property on Wood Island, a working-class, tree-lined neighborhood, was sold out from under my Italian maternal great-grandparents for the ever-expanding Logan Airport. The South End and the North End were carved up for the Central Artery, and the West End, where my Albanian paternal grandparents lived, was destroyed for the spread of Mass General Hospital. My father, five at the time, remembers running up and down the girders that lined his narrow street.

My family scattered. My father's went to Somerville and my mother's to East Boston. Constant change is the story of our Boston: generations of people on the move, retelling, revising, and rebuilding as life careened off the rails. My Grammy Duca, my mother's mother, lived on thirteen streets in East Boston. My mother, even more.

Wonderland presaged the changes in Boston that were coming to rip out our hearts and homes. Everything changes, and that's the way it's going to be, Kid. No crying about it.

And although the Wonderland Amusement Park is long gone, the name lives on. If you asked my family about Wonderland, they'd tell you it's the last stop on Boston's Blue line. Or that the Wonderland dog track was where all the mobsters got shot. Or they'd direct you to the Wonderland Bus Depot, where my uncle towed broken buses from across Boston. They might remember my Grammy Duca dancing at Wonderland Ballroom in the 1950s, a single mother of five with a drunk and deadbeat husband. Maybe they'd tell you about the roller coaster on the beach, but even then, it would be to tell you it burned—that it's gone now too, like so much else.

The thing about Wonderland is how my family, the city, and various historical societies and websites treated it like magic, its influence much bigger than its brief existence. Wonderland was grand and worthy of belonging to a place called Revere. The park may have been lost to history, but we still felt its shine. We all dreamed big and sparking dreams that rotated slowly past us.

And while Wonderland was barely there, the truth of the place remains: For a hardscrabble bunch of Bostonians—working class, immigrants, and descendants of immigrants—it was comforting to think there was a time when our world shimmered with growth and opportunity. The whole beach lit up.

My Boston was full of thieves and stickup guys. It was a town that believed the streets taught the only lessons you should learn, since books couldn't shoot you dead. It was a place where if you got took, it's on you, buddy. You shoulda known *bettah*. We were Wonderland too. Spectacular, lit up by hope and fantasy.

THIS PLACE USED TO BE WONDERLAND

My father, Phil, outside the Treska family home on Hancock Street, Somerville, August 2015

n **August 2015,** I visited my father, Phil, in Boston for the weekend. My aunt Loretta, his older sister, had died that February, the coldest on record. That winter, the temperature barely broke the single digits. Phil had come home for Loretta's funeral but refused to divulge the specifics of the service to me, insisting it was too cold and too sad. I wanted to respect his request, and I wanted to protect myself from guilt, so I listened to him. He stayed at a hotel because his only remaining sibling, my uncle Bobby, didn't offer a room.

I lived in New York City and went to Boston every year on the cheapest Chinatown bus I could find, risking my life up and down the Mass Turnpike. Out my rainy window, I saw Boston on the horizon. It was a summer storm, and fat drops lazed in streaks and webs across the glass. The city looked small compared to how it existed in my memory. Its cluster of downtown buildings—the Pru, the John Hancock, and the Custom House Tower—dwarfed by Boston Harbor and Logan Airport. On a rainy day, the harbor spread into the sky.

When Phil told me he'd be in Boston for his annual checkup at the Lahey Clinic in Burlington, I told him I'd meet him there.

The bus docked inside South Station, and I made my way through the crowded depot lined with floor-to-ceiling windows. Peter Pan, Greyhound, Lucky Star, Megabus, and Coach USA buses idled with their luggage docks open, gaping mouths waiting to be stuffed. Leaving out the side door, I circumvented the traffic in front and found my dad standing outside his rental car, waving in a Patriots sweatshirt. He stood with his weight on his good leg. His bad knee turned sideways, made so by grenade shrapnel in Vietnam and a long-overdue knee replacement.

Phil lived off his VA benefits in Florida. For surviving that grenade, the United States government paid him three thousand dollars a month. This was enough for the rent and bills, with leftovers to visit his kids; cheap beers by the pool; a girlfriend or two or three. He spent his days on the beach until his skin was purple-brown. He'd been bald since before I was born—a horseshoe of hair below a gleaming dome. My papa, Christie Treska, and my uncles, Dennis and Bobby, they had that hairline too. Coronated as a Treska, I have a bald spot at the crown of my head. Tall with broad shoulders, Phil posed like a bodybuilder or a prisoner in photos—chest out, hands balled into fists. No matter the frame, Phil ducked down with loads of sky behind him. He was still handsome and earned his slow and tilting strut.

Hobbling over to squeeze me too hard, he told me to get in the car. I had a curly auburn bob; blue eyes, almost gray; and a mole over my left eyebrow. I had my dad's broad shoulders and was only a few inches shorter, wearing a tie-dyed maxi dress, Birkenstocks, and a bright blue American Apparel hoodie. I did as I was told and threw my leather duffel in the back seat. We were off.

"So you got it made, huh, Kid? Off all week? Very nice. Who you got paying the rent? You making that *para?*"

Para meant cash. It was one of the only Albanian words we knew anymore. My great-grandfather, Baba Treska, brought his children to America one at a time. He earned the money selling fruits and vegetables from his cart in Haymarket Square, outside Faneuil Hall. My papa arrived in 1932, when he was fifteen. By the time I was born, only the essential made it through. The other word I knew was *besa*, because my papa whispered to us in Albanian about loyalty and love.

"I sure am. There's a couple from Costa Rica staying at the house. They leave the day before I get back."

In January, my roommate of six years had moved in with his girlfriend. Then, the new lease arrived and my rent increased from $1,800 to $2,100 a month. I couldn't keep up on my own.

I'd seen Airbnb advertised on the subway, promising extra cash for your spare bed. The website presented a solution to my problems. I could host tourists looking for a cheaper night's sleep in a big city or an authentic neighborhood experience. I read the testimonials as the train rocked me through dark tunnels and up into daylight. I decided to rent out my spare room.

It didn't seem *that* strange. I had moved to Manhattan months after the 2008 economic crash. The cost of living went up 25 percent in my first five years in the city. I went into $50,000 of student debt to afford to start my life. On poverty's constant edge, I was a steampipe building with nowhere to blow. And I wasn't alone.

Airbnb listings in New York City peaked in 2015, hitting

nearly fifty thousand available units. The site was founded the same year I moved to New York; the same year the housing market collapsed. But it took years for the effects of the crash to create the need for Americans to supplement our income by monetizing discrete parts of our lives. To gig economy. By the time my roommate moved out, I made my living off short-term labor and dated short-term lovers off the dating apps, so why not have short-term roommates too? One of my mentors, Professor Reynolds, called the hustle "quilting a life together." And that was what I was doing, frantically sewing scraps.

I was an adjunct instructor at The City College of New York and taught as many undergraduate English classes as I could secure. The semester didn't start for another two weeks, which usually meant months without pay. Adjunct paychecks followed the academic calendar, and getting paid on time was always a struggle. Even though we made up 60 percent of the college's teaching payroll, we were seen as off-the-totem-pole insignificant.

Class assignments were demoralizing too. Departments overpromised and underdelivered. Classes were given like a gift, or canceled last minute. And the pay was shit. It was one of those "you should be happy to be here" kind of jobs. If I taught eight classes a year, I made under thirty thousand dollars in New York City. I called us the waitresses of academia. It felt accurate enough, except I made way more money as a waitress.

Hosting tourists addressed the cash shortage I'd known my whole life. I had a good system down for renting. I stayed for check-in, introduced my guests to the apartment and its "charming" quirks, gave them my contact information, then headed out for the weekend, somewhere close in case something went wrong.

Forever dazzled by cash, Phil was intrigued. His face danced with wonder.

"Strangers staying in your house while you're away. You ever worry you're gonna get ripped off?"

"Every day. But I'm making so much money that if they rob me, 'Here, take it. I've got too much.'"

I shoved my valuables at an invisible European paying my rent. My dad laughed.

"All right, all right. You got me. Let 'em have it."

I made thousands a month. And believe me when I tell you: never in my life had I made that kind of money. My guests paid my whole rent in two weeks, and the rest went into my checking account. August was typically when I lurked around the English department, but this year I was on vacation. I told my dad that after the Costa Rican couple left, a Norwegian couple would check in and stay two weeks. Then, a woman from France for five days. I paid for our hotel in Gloucester, the idyllic fishing town north of Boston where we were headed for the weekend.

As we made our way toward Somerville, he mused about his sister's funeral. "Snowbanks taller than the car the night we buried her."

Auntie Loretta was a paranoid schizophrenic, among other diagnoses. She was psychotic, obsessive compulsive, manic depressive. She had it all. My poor auntie. She spent the last twenty years of her long, miserable life institutionalized. By the time she died at seventy-five, she swore and snarled racisms at the men and women who worked in the mental hospital.

She said they abused her. Phil said it was impossible to distinguish abuse from restraint. I was proud of her for dying in a maelstrom, for manifesting a cold accurate enough to die in.

"I wanted to be there for her," I told him.

"She knows you loved her, Nicole."

That was all either of us said about it. I thought my auntie probably loved the idea of me and my sister. Maybe even the idea of Phil, her younger brother. She hadn't seen any of us in a long time. Lindsay and I saw Auntie Loretta only when we visited on weekends, in the summer, and over the holidays. We got older and went home less and less. Phil didn't know what to do with his sister's steep decline, so he did what he knew best: he found the door and skedaddled to Florida. We're a family full of runners from a city of runners. We get the fuck out of there. We move and set up somewhere safe and make ourselves real until we have to do it again.

We passed the old Boston Garden, now the TD Garden (it will always only be "the Garden" to me). I saw Larry Bird and the Celtics play there in the eighties, when they were gods. My stepdad took me and a boy from Brunswick, Maine, who lived down the street from us on the navy base. His father died in a strange accident with the platoon in Iceland. I sat close to the broken boy on our broken seats, and we watched Larry Bird lope up and down the parquet.

When they tore the old Garden down in 1998, they exposed its famous floor and columns to the cars coming into the city and it felt cheap.

Phil drove us over the Bunker Hill Bridge, which stretched across the water like a wishbone necklace. Then we were out of Boston proper and into the swirling trap of on-ramps and off-ramps that cradled Boston Sand & Gravel, a beloved city landmark. I think it's a very Boston thing, to love a concrete company. Giant belts shook and popped with gravel and rocks that climbed and climbed into god knew what kind of grinder before getting spit out the other side, a fine and shifting mountain.

We passed Bunker Hill Community College. Phil went there for a semester after it opened, not long after he returned from Vietnam.

"You know it was a jail before it was a college?" Phil said.

The community college stood on the grounds of the old Charlestown State Prison, which closed in 1955. The governor called it "a bastille that eclipses in infamy any current prison in the United States." The college bore no mark of the prison that came before.

"That's where they executed Sacco and Vanzetti," my dad told me. Boston's history of violence was long and storied. Its reformatories, prisons, and asylums were renowned and renounced for their sadism, but not until long after the damage was done.

"Well, an institution's an institution's an institution, I suppose," I said.

"And we're all in the madhouse, Kid," he shot back, laughing at his own joke.

Phil loved to take I-93 through the city. It was a family point of pride to drive past Mass General, Storrow Drive, the West End, the North End, East Boston, and say: *I was born right there.* The only understanding you could have of Boston was a deeply personal one; otherwise, you were a tourist.

We were on our way to Hancock Street, where my father

and his family had lived. To Magoun Square, more of a triangle than a square, where Broadway and Medford Street intersected. My papa's diner, Christie's, sat on Medford Street and once hosted the entire Winter Hill Gang, the Irish arm of the mob syndicate that controlled Boston through the sixties, seventies, and eighties. They set up their enemies with the feds and consolidated power. They ran books and armed the IRA and engaged in your typical mob-type behavior: racketeering, robbery, drugs, murder. They converged on my papa's diner late into the night.

Most infamous among his clientele were mob bosses Howie Winter and Whitey Bulger. Howie was from Somerville and came to power in 1965 after the Irish Mob Wars killed or jailed most of his contemporaries. Whitey, from Southie, took over in 1978. Whitey was legend. He did time in Alcatraz. His brother was a state senator. There are movies about him. He controlled the Winter Hill Gang, the FBI, and the city of Boston with a calculating intensity until his indictment in 1994, when he disappeared. He spent sixteen years on the run.

Which is all to say, at my papa's diner there were booths reserved for the most dangerous criminals in the city. Maybe the country.

My dad worked at Christie's after Vietnam. On the griddle, Phil felt a clarity he hadn't felt since boot camp at Parris Island. He pumped out omelets and egg-and-cheese sandwiches at all hours, clean on the plate. Phil short-ordered to order his mind. Treskas know a few things: we can cook, we can fight, and we can fuck—we should have it glorious, with innate talent like that. Yet we toil and burn like everyone else.

Christie's location in Winter Hill made it a favorite for

Howie and Whitey, but my papa served all the gangsters in Boston. He respected them. He pointed his own sons, and even his daughter, to break on organized crime's rocky shores. He set his children toward shipwreck. Young and beautiful once, my auntie Loretta sailed around the restaurant, waiting tables and having affairs with the handsome, handsy mobsters who came, went, and turned up dead.

To the Treska family, gangs were benevolent. Many of the earners and business owners believed the Winter Hill Gang was worth the cost they exacted. My papa certainly saw them as respectable. He saw his booths fill with patrons and his bank account fill with money, and he considered his affiliation with the Winter Hill Gang successful.

What was there to say? Criminals ran Boston. There were only so many paths a person could take on this earth and in that town, so what was wrong with a little money and security? And not for nothing, but if you ran the numbers, you'd find yourself with a pretty strong argument regarding the pursuit of criminal pursuits in America. To be in a gang was to be respected and feared. To be legitimized. There was nothing petty about the mob. Nothing poor.

I knew my papa had a diner. I did not know it had been a hangout for some of Boston's most notorious mobsters or that my papa, the old Albanian boxer, was their hero. I didn't know that the Winter Hill Gang had grown along with my papa; that my papa's successes, and my father's too, were tied to the mob.

After I found out, I subscribed to the *Boston Globe* archives to dig around for our names. I found a 1967 article that listed my papa as one of "seven alleged badmen," their forte illegal gambling. He went to trial for racketeering. I read the list of names to my father, and he laughed and said, "Shit, Nicole, I grew up with those guys at Papa's diner. That's every bookie in Boston right there."

I reached out to the research librarian at the Boston Public Library, and he found it strange that the paper never recorded the outcome of the case. What kind of friends in what kinds of offices pulled those kinds of strings? The ones that make things disappear? Some things will remain secret.

My family members were bit parts in a bigger picture, walk-ons, supporting cast. But they'd be the first to tell you they were in the shot. Our pedigree was proxy: one degree removed from first. My parents knew who buried the bodies, and that knowing was currency to many in Boston, a passport through a world with tight borders.

That said, I think I know what my papa couldn't know until his heart exploded in the hallway on Hancock Street: the Winter Hill Gang giveth, the Winter Hill Gang taketh away. All our Treska lives and deaths were caught up in the gang's long reach.

The diner burned to the ground after my papa died in 1987. My uncle Bobby locked up and strolled across the street to the hardware store. By the time he came out, the diner was engulfed. Oranges and reds sky-high. Nothing he could do about it, he said.

IN BOSTON, I HAD THE uncanny feeling of being a sleepwalker. The city changed so much and so fast that it was perplexing even to lifelong residents. It should have made me feel better that both my family members and I felt certain there used to be a bridge here or a tunnel there, but they had a different claim to their ignorance. They lived through the Big Dig, and I was just a dummy hick who left too soon and lost her accent. What did I know about home anymore?

But I knew about Boston.

Boston was Beansie, who lost his eye playing darts at the bar. He tied a long string to the barrel and pulled the dart back from the board one time too many.

Boston was the Marathon bombers, those brothers who used pressure cookers for bombs, like they knew some grim joke, some innate truth about the place, though they'd be labeled outsiders.

Boston was Ha-Ha's husband, who knocked off banks in strip malls all over Charlestown, a town of bank robbers. He and his crew smashed and grabbed tens of thousands of dollars before they got caught and did a handful at Walpole, the maximum-security prison.

Boston was the stewardess who smuggled drugs for the mob. A neighborhood girl, my mother always said, just like us. One day, a balloon burst in her stomach and she dropped dead outside Logan. That's what happened—people lived right up until they died.

Boston was Patty Eggplant, named after the discovery that the parm she brought to my first birthday party was not hers, but her mother's. The nickname was a reminder that you never lived it down, not where we came from.

Boston was the loom and the yoke and the wheel that broke you. It was every kind of cancer spreading all at once; it was in your bones, your heart, your lungs.

Boston was me, though I didn't go there anymore. The

place pulled from my heart never-ending, like a magician with one of those rainbow scarves. And even after decades gone, the bones remained to point the way.

Didn't I used to be here in a different way?

We did. We all did.

When I said I could walk myself home without a map, I meant it. Every time I landed at Logan and saw the red-and-white water tower at the Soldiers' Home, I cried. It's gone now.

When we hit Broadway, I knew we were in Winter Hill before I saw the sign for the bakery. In the 1970s, the bakery was Pal Joey's, the barroom headquarters of Howie's. When Phil wasn't manning the griddle, he ran the books for the neighborhood, taking bets from all the gamblers and wiseguys around town. He made his drops at Pal Joey's once a week, where he dumped his cash onto a pool table already covered in cash. We passed the bakery, descended Winter Hill, and turned left at the Dunkin' Donuts on Cedar Street.

We parked across from the house on Hancock Street and got out of the car. Phil walked down the driveway, which used to be two long strips of concrete with grass overgrown on all sides. When Lindsay and I visited our dad, Cadillacs filled the driveway, paid for by the diner and whichever family member's particular vices: racketeering, gambling, or stealing. For years after his death, Uncle Dennis's '74 Escalade sat there, dead as he was. The summer sun cracked the seats and the dash; the winter cold blasted the once-galactic paint dull.

The low garage barely fit a car and smelled like damp earth and oil. I spent hours in there doing bad-kid stuff, lit only by the filtered sun through the dirty windows.

The little backyard was hedged by raspberry bushes my

auntie Loretta planted before I was born. In the summer, we sat around plastic pools in beach chairs that folded in thirds and had mechanics that clicked and pinched. They were so beautiful—desirable eighties neon colors woven over flimsy aluminum frames. They made me bleed and scream, but the feel on my legs and butt as I slid around was worth the pain of the dismount. There were good times.

On rare days off, my papa loved to barbecue shirtless in the yard, an Igloo of beers beside him. The terror he was to the boys, he wasn't ever to Loretta or us grandbabies. By the time we came along, he handed out hamburgers on the weekends, and bloodred Orthodox eggs on Easter. He had parakeets.

My grandmother Louise was mean and hard and crazy as ever when we turned up. She didn't get soft until she had a stroke at Mass General in 1994, the hospital built over the neighborhood where she was born. Her whole life, she tormented her husband and children with her accusations and paranoia, Loretta worst of all. And Louise got worse with age, the way some women do. Men get soft and die a charm, and women get hard and die made of wood. Sometimes it's like that.

My auntie Loretta may have been the only certifiably insane person in the family, but believe you me, everyone was mad in their own way.

In the year she lived between strokes, my father's mother was so kind. She couldn't speak, but her face softened into the excitement of a child when we visited her in the hospital. She was tiny, foregrounded against a spray of hoses. She waved us into her open arms. I saw her, then, as a little girl from the West End.

The following year, in 1995, Phil and Bobby sold the house on Hancock Street and split the $240,000 three ways. Auntie Loretta was prone to psychotic episodes, and after my grandparents died, she started her life inside. She moved from mental home to mental home. Her share of the house and inheritance went to providing her the best care her brothers could find. When put that way, it made a lot of sense. But that wasn't all. The ghosts and death and insanity weren't the only reasons they split the money and split. There were tales of insurance fraud, of gambling debts. There were tales of fire and flames. A Boston classic.

When I questioned Phil about Hancock Street, his response was always, *It was our house, and we needed the money.* Phil's need for money often ended in gone houses, gone christening checks and child support. I was angry into adulthood that my father didn't include Lindsay and me in his decision to sell the house, but now I see that he did: dads are more likely to stick around when they're not on the run, and they're not on the run when they pay their gambling debts. By and large, my dad was around.

Back on the sidewalk, I looked down Hancock Street.

"I remember getting beat up around here when I was little," I said.

"A real Treska tradition. I did a lot of beating up too."

"Yeah, I remember you doing a lot of that," I said.

My mom left when I was almost three. Phil slapped her into the fridge when she was pregnant with Lindsay, and I didn't even look up from my toy xylophone. I used to cry or hide. In those days, he was drunk in the daytime and wore a gun on his ankle. One night my mom took us to my uncle Stanley's house—he was a cop—and we didn't come back.

Was my mom alone in this? Not by a long shot. All those aunties and cousins across all those neighborhoods of Boston? All those kitchen tables loaded with shrimp cocktail, meatballs and gravy, sausage and peppers. What do you think they talked about for hours, years, entire lives? Drinking their coffee and sambuca, dunking their biscotti and perfect little anise cookies with the rainbow sprinkles? And I mean no disrespect to the husbands of Somerville and East Boston who didn't slap their wives around. I'm sure they were legion, too, but I didn't know them very well.

Phil hadn't meant *those* beatings. The ones when he rag-dolled my mom around. We didn't talk about them much. When we did, he never denied it, but he changed the subject.

"Nicole, take some pictures. Come on."

I let him because I forgave my father.

We opened the chain-link gate like we still lived there and sat on the chipped gray porch. I remember when the paint poured so thick over the wooden planks that the seams pooled. I played on my belly with my parents' and my grandparents' screen doors open, those cheap metal ones that slammed with purpose.

Yes, darkness lived at Hancock Street, but so did safety and light.

"Here, Dad. Stay put, and I'll take your picture."

I hopped off the steps and down the concrete walkway.

At the sight of the camera, Phil moved to the center of the frame. He pulled his USMC hat out of his back pocket and put it over his bald head.

"Do I look okay?" he asked, earnest and insecure.

How did he get so vain?

I lined him up between the two white pillars of our child-

27

hood and let him get comfortable. He rested his bad leg down the steps and ran his hands down the front of his unbuttoned aloha-print shirt. He straightened his back and shook himself out. I took a few shots and gave him a thumbs-up.

"Okay," he said, "let me get you now."

He rocked himself onto his good leg. I gave him my phone and sat on the porch, my hands shoved in the pockets of my hoodie. I learned how to ride my bike outside that chain-link fence, a pink two-wheeler with training wheels and long plastic streamers that *thwip-thwipp*ed in the wind. I remember the way the new rubber on the wheels smelled. I smiled and my dad poked the phone with his finger a few times. He hobbled up to show me the screen.

"Look good?" he asked.

Before I could answer, he interjected. "Great. Let's get out of here before I get too sad."

•

AUNTIE LORETTA USED TO TAKE us to Star Market, a twenty-minute walk down Central Street. We'd start off after she finished the various chores my grandmother assigned to fill her days. Auntie Loretta waved at the old-timers on their porches, and they called, *Say hello to your mother and father.* She speculated on the quiet houses, fantastic theories in a hush; Lindsay and me, still small, were riveted.

To get to the market, we had to cross Central Street, one of Somerville's major thoroughfares. Seeing my auntie stop traffic with authority made me confident in her, no matter the strange things she said about outer space. We walked into Star Market, and the cashiers and bag boys yelled *Hello, Lo-*

retta! They flirted her in and out the door. On the corner, we stopped by the Italian ice cart and walked home slowly and carefully with lemon and cherry dripping from our elbows.

Back at Hancock Street, Auntie Loretta gave my sister and me baths. She used a bar of soap as shampoo; there was no conditioner upstairs at my grandparents'. We sat in the tub while my aunt ran the bar back and forth across the crowns of our heads. It wasn't soft, but it was love: purposeful and cleansing, hard but for your own good. We winced. When we were done, Auntie sat on the toilet and held us between her thighs, running the comb through our soap-tangled hair.

We never cried. She was doing us a kindness and being more careful with us than you could ever hope for anyone to be with another person. She was full of love that she poured rough onto us. I don't even think that was her mental illness. I think that was her Treska. We only know how to love rough. It's the only way we've been loved.

My auntie's moles sprouted hairs out of their centers, and her chin bristled with stiff stubble. We loved her, but we recoiled from her kisses, which scratched. It was hurtful to her, but we did it nevertheless. My grandmother had whiskers, too, but she was mean, so feeling repulsed came easy.

Lindsay and I grew up inside Loretta's fantastical thinking. Whether we were little birds getting our scalps scrubbed off in the bathtub or snuggled next to her in the sunroom after her appointments, we heard it all.

Those days were so natural, running errands in the city with Auntie Loretta. It never felt crazy or unsafe, but it must have been. There must have been questions of proportion.

Everyone except us kids knew Loretta wasn't in her right mind.

But we weren't stupid. Our time on the sidewalk and in the sunroom was not lost on me or my sister. We heard it all. We talked about it downstairs in our shared bedroom. Mars sounded good, but did we think her doctor could save us spots on the shuttle? The old man on the corner with the Scottish terrier and the Kangol hat? Was he a spy? He looked nicer than our papa and gave us candy. Auntie said we could take it, but only so he didn't put our name on a list or report us for suspicious activity. We kids nodded sagely, sucked our candy suspiciously.

When my auntie talked about a baby, we wondered about that too, but in the same way that we wondered about the neighbors and spaceships. Phil never spoke of Loretta's past. Instead, he went uncharacteristically quiet. Phil spoke to fill silence, to shove off memories and uncertainties.

My auntie was a beautiful girl who turned into a crazy woman with toothpaste on her shirt and lipstick on her teeth. She talked to herself and left the gas on. She was dangerous, but she loved me. My whole life I heard tales of her heartache: breakups and breakdowns, the trips to Vegas and Phil's boot camp; electroshock therapies that didn't do any good but kept coming and coming. She had a laugh like mine, but hoarser, from smoking and disuse.

All I know about Loretta young is that she fell in love and then fell apart, over and over. I understood that. But I didn't know the exact story. The children of secrets become adults of best guesses. All I've got is my *must've*s and *probably*s.

So when Lindsay and I went through our days with Loretta,

guessing at likelihoods, I fear we would've marked Loretta's memories as untrue. Or maybe fantasy—a story in the realm of the unbelievable, like a book. It was hard to see youth in the woman in front of us at the tub, her bar of soap crossing hard one way and back the other. It seemed more likely that our auntie would end up on a mission to Mars than someone's someone. Someone's mother, lover, waitress.

•

PHIL AND I LEFT HANCOCK Street and crossed the Mystic River, near where Phil used to sell used cars after he got out of prison. On my summer and winter breaks from school, he'd pick me up in the company Caddy and take me to a fluorescent-lit diner off the parkway that made the best steak and cheese subs. We would eat the subs and confirm their goodness, our goodness, to each other in the falling night.

Phil drove south along the edge of Everett and Chelsea, industrial waterfronts and potholed streets, mountains of salt and gravel. Traffic was heavy with Mack trucks. We crossed the Chelsea Canal into East Boston.

East Boston, where the pignoli, tricolori, and biscotti were piled high and brilliant in display cases. Where Scali bread jiggled through bread slicers, raining seeds; where the scent of imported ham and grated Romano fattened the air of the corner stores, soaked into the gappy hardwood, and seeped onto the sidewalk. East Boston, under the flight path into Logan, where the jets dragged their fat bellies over the rooftops every five minutes.

East Boston was where my mom, Christine, was from. She met Phil there in 1977. She had a thing for bad boys in gold chains. Phil thought my mom was a cute little redhead with a mouth on her. He took her for a ride on the back of his motorcycle, and they kissed on that dirty little beach at the end of Thurston Street in Orient Heights.

"Can we drive past the pub and Barnes Avenue?" I asked my dad.

Barnes Avenue was the last apartment my grammy Duca, my mother's mother, lived in before the assisted living home off Route 1 in Saugus. The Barnes Avenue apartment backed up to the Orient Heights T station. Across Saratoga Street was the Victory Pub, where my mother's baby brother, my uncle Bone, worked as a line cook. When it was slow, he chain-smoked on a folding chair and read the *Globe*.

Before I was born, Uncle Bone burned down a triple-decker. He was living with my mom and fell asleep drunk with a cigarette. One too many times. When I was a toddler, he used to take me to the park on Thurston Street. He played handball in denim shorts as the planes came in. He belted the words to "Lola," by the Kinks, and slapped the rubber ball against the concrete wall. He met its return fast and then again, his swing animated, his palm tough from the impact. East Boston was a gray place with hard edges.

"Sure," Phil said. "We'll go up the Heights, then head out to Winthrop and Revere. We'll do the whole tour before we head to Gloucester. How 'bout it?"

"It's the Nicole Treska *This Is Your Life!* " I said. "It's fun and funny and also full of sad stuff this place won't let you forget."

Phil brought us around the front of the Victory Pub, which was shuttered, though its sign still hung long from the second floor. Then, Donna's Restaurant—my mother went to high school with Donna—and across the street, Ruggiero's Funeral Parlor. I knew Ruggiero's as a place that stole parking spots from Donna's on the weekends, until we buried my grammy there and it became something else entirely. We pulled into the central strip of parking spots, traffic coming and going on either narrow side.

Phil waved his hand around the neighborhood: the T tracks, the five-way intersection, Grammy's old house, all the storefronts of my youth laid out like a play.

"You, from this place, can you believe it!"

He said it like he hadn't already said it a million, trillion times.

We laughed at the little irony that I, the child who read books and got arrested only once, came from this cradle. It was a joke that could offend me, depending on which family member said it and their tone. From my dad, though, the joke came from a place of deep understanding of his daughter and his city.

As a teenager, I arrived in Boston with a nose piercing, an ankle tattoo, hairy armpits, and corduroy-patched pants with torn and dirty hems from getting dragged around concert parking lots. I was ungainly in the nineties—a chubby teenager with the hormonal emergence of dark body hair and moles that indicated my Albanian ethnicity. In high school, my family remarked on what a pretty child I'd been.

Grammy Duca loved me best, and on her deathbed in 2013, when she was eighty-two and I was thirty-three, I lay with her and said, "Oh, Grammy, what if I'm not enough?"

And she said, "Baby, you've always been more than enough, don't you know that?"

I didn't know. I wish she could've seen that I finally *had* enough—enough money to pay my rent, save, and travel. I wanted to tell her that those years of struggle aided my understanding that I was, in fact, enough. And I wasn't being shallow. Money wasn't everything, but paid bills and full fridges changed everything. The money I spent on shelf-stable foods I could spend, instead, on fresh vegetables. (*Use this money to buy canned food*, my grammy's note read in neat cursive. And I did.) I didn't know how long my own good fortune would last, but out of knee-jerk townie suspiciousness, I feared it couldn't be long.

"All right, you get a good look around, Kid?" Phil said. "You want to head to Revere?"

He pulled his good leg back inside the rental and then, with both hands and gingerly, his bad one. Driving limos in the city made him quick and heavy on the brake, and his age was starting to show behind the wheel and in all the other ways.

Above us, the Madonna, Queen of the Universe Shrine sat hidden in her tower, and passenger jets skipped across paper rooftops on their way to the harbor. East Boston. Water on all sides. To this very day, whenever I pass a neighborhood near auto repair shops or city bus hangars, refineries or natural gas storage tanks, I think: *Ahh, I'm home.*

PHIL AND I HIT REVERE Beach Parkway. The annual sand-sculpture festival lined the wide beach in a fixed parade. At the Winthrop end, 1970s-style condos piled up, evidence of the last swell of development before the blizzard of '78. Shingled houses sat in stubborn rows facing the water, and American flags whipped and snapped in the wind spit by the Atlantic. Nahant peninsula was visible in the distance, and the beach crumbled toward the oblivion of the shore.

"You know where we are, Kid?" Phil asked.

The seawall ran the length of the bay, wide enough for two people lying longways, beach chairs, and coolers. On the best summer days, it was miles of skin: old men holding suncatchers rotated slow like satellites; women in flip-flops, with tanning accelerator and boom boxes; kids who ran and leaped.

"Of course I know where I am!"

My mother was very pregnant with me in the summer of 1979, and weeks overdue, she tipped her way down the broad steps at Revere Beach. She dug down until the sand was cool and rested her globe of a stomach, her giant, tender breasts.

When we were kids, Lindsay and I played paddleball on the beach while our mother and her best friend, Henball, drank vodka lemonades from the seawall above. They chain-smoked and got sun-drunk. We imitated the women—hands on our hips, shoulders back—six, seven, eight years old and already foulmouthed, neck-jerking little hip swivelers. Henball applied layer after layer of *Bain De Soleil* Orange Gelee tanning lotion; my mother wore a wide-brimmed hat. We were made of time.

Because I didn't go home often, my family treated me as if I'd never been there at all, shocked when I recognized a landmark or knew where I was. I took my tongue and unbroke it. I said *car* and *horse* and *here* and *there* with the articulation of a nonregional newscaster. The cost was going home an absolute disgrace. Questions I got from my family: *Who do you think you are? Who's better than you? You think you're so smart?*

My father lived with my uncle Bobby on Revere Beach until my parents got married. I know this because whenever we drove the strip (which in a Boston lifetime is a number impossible to count), Phil pointed to the unit and told me the stories.

"Hey, isn't that where Henball's boyfriend got murdered?" I said, pointing to a different building facing the shore. I liked to hear the stories as much as my dad liked to tell them, so I prompted him as he pulled into a parking spot.

"Oh, shit, you remember that?" my father said, parking the car. "You were a baby when that happened. A nice guy, the professor. He was at your christening."

When I was a baby, my mother worked in the North End with Bianca and Henball. Henball was dating a professor—a tall guy with dark curls and natural brawn who lived on Revere Beach. He was the kind of guy my uncles and cousins fought after the bars closed; whose abandoned couch became my cousin's summer score. Bianca was married to a notorious hit man, Joey. Joey was a madman with no fidelity except to himself. He made massacres all around town. He'd kill his mother for cocaine.

The professor, though, he was a criminal too. Fresh out of Walpole, and he set himself up dealing coke to his faculty friends.

"A real nice guy," Phil said, shading his eyes and looking into the past, as one does at Revere Beach. "I never understood why he hung around with all those wiseguys."

Joey turned up to the professor's apartment with his goons one Friday night, and murdered him by Sunday. Joey never got the drugs, but they were mostly pretense. His appetite for violence was growing along with his gut and he was making a big fat mess out of everything. And he liked it that way. I imagine the professor knew early into their weekend together how things would end, whether he gave up the coke or not. I knew two minutes into the first time I heard the story as a kid. These stories all end the same.

"I hung around with those guys. And I knew they were fucking animals. But the professor? He didn't know. Your mother? She still doesn't know."

As a baby, I was passed around and kissed by these maniacs and murderers—*What a little angel*—and here's what I know: no one saw it coming when Joey came for them. Joey was beyond a hit man. At least a hit man has some kind of ethic.

Listen up: neither book smarts nor street smarts can save you from a chaos among us.

"You told me, Pops," I said. He'd told me a million times. I thought about my parents, young and doing their best to stay alive in a world that ate itself to death every day.

That was why people from our side of the Charles thought people on the other side of the Charles were stupid, no matter their degree. My mother often said things like, "Book smarts are nice, but I'll take street smarts, thank you very much. Any idiot can read a book, but can you read a situation? Can you read the streets?"

My uncle Stanley, a detective with the Boston Police Department's drug unit, worked the professor's homicide.

Of course I knew where I was.

ALONG THE BEACH, ARTISTS STOOD on ladders and inside deep depressions to create sculptures out of sand. They wore hats and used small brushes and pinky fingers to smooth and define.

We got out of the car and made our way to Kelly's Roast Beef, right in the middle of the beach, right in the middle of the action. Kelly's was *it*—monumental. Revered and surrounded by congregants. As both a city rat and a navy brat, I was comfortable in crowded places. I enjoyed being where the people were. I never felt alone in a crowd. If there was a line, I wanted to be in it.

The wind and small waves created a background static that insulated us. We were in the deep in the ever-present line, and I was at home.

"Did they get a new sign?" I yelled, my neck craning toward the neon KELLY's looming above us, green and not yet lit for the night. Above the walkup windows, photographs and clean type announced the menu. I remembered blue snap-on letter boards and hand-drawn hot dogs. Something older than neon. Or did I? How could I know? Over a lifetime, it was hard to say exactly what changed and what stayed the same. Too many questions were an indictment.

"Same sign," my father said, lost in the menu: fried oyster platter, lobster roll, roast beef sandwich, fried clams, cheese fries, fish sandwich. He considered the choices with the élan of an old man on cholesterol blockers.

Neither the place nor the menu had changed much in either of our lives, but going to Kelly's was still an occasion. The counter girls punched computer screens, and behind them, the line cooks performed their endless and fluid hustle. Orders on orange trays slid out of the pickup window, clean.

We sat under a canopy of seagulls encouraging us to eat

quickly. Revere Beach belonged to the seagulls. They plucked sandwiches from the hands of the unguarded or the weak, and they shit on everything. Their caw, high and sharp, was not unlike the thick accents of East Boston, Winthrop, Saugus, Revere, Somerville, Chelsea, Southie, Lynn. The *Hey, Kids* and the *How's your mutha?*'s called from window to seawall, from seawall to sidewalk, mixed familiar and easy with the avian squawks above.

Roast beef sandwiches are a specialty of the North Shore. Thinly shaved roast beef piled on a seeded, buttered bun (for my money, be it with hot dog or burger or roast beef, the buttered griddle bun is close to God) and a tangy orange barbecue sauce that's too runny to be considered a barbecue sauce most anywhere else.

The sidewalk was sandy and sticky, and no one wore much in the way of clothing or sunscreen. Children pleaded for jimmies in front of soft-serve ice cream trucks. Their mothers held buckets and babies and sandals. A handful of boys stood waist-high in the ocean, their skinny legs wrapped in brown-green ribbons of kelp and algae. Seagulls pitched and rolled in the wind.

Phil and I faced the water with our feet dangling over the drop and watched the artists on the beach. They crafted castles, mermaids, ships, and squid; all the saints and heroes of the Catholic Church, American Revolution, and Boston Red Sox. The sculptures looked like slabs of stone, but really they were bits of busted-up quartz and shell made stable under pressure somehow. A wonder.

The Atlantic was almost gray that day, the color of cold. Some days it turned a steely blue that looked startling, but even then it wasn't inviting.

"Look, you can't even hang on the beach anymore," Phil said as he swept his hand across the sculpture superhighway to highlight the audacity.

"As if you ever hang on the beach anymore." I elbowed him and rattled the ice in my cup, trying to get to the bottom of it.

I wondered if things were so much better before. Or if, as time and life slid away over the Atlantic, we didn't yearn for the volume of the past—its capacity to hold hope. There was always tension when I came home, and it shimmered in the air along with the heat. Historical signs tacked to the seawall apologized: *This place used to be Wonderland.*

"You can't even step off the sidewalk into the sand with that knee. Have you called your doctor yet?"

Phil's knee replacement was twenty years too old. He was afraid to end up dead on the table if he replaced it again and said Vietnam couldn't kill him all these years later. Because family news was rarely good, I stayed behind. I let calls go to voicemail.

"I called my doctor at the Lahey. I'll go in and get it checked out. But you don't understand, Nicole. The old man was doing his best, and with Loretta, I got distracted. You know, I got lost in Loretta and my guilt and my own shit. And now Lindsay needs me. Have you talked to your sister? Did she tell you I'm going to Colorado for Christmas, and maybe I'm going to stay awhile?"

My dad was talking about my little sister's life falling apart in a suburb outside Denver. She couldn't afford the mortgage because her husband, Frank, was using.

"She called and said she found Frank high again. They're trying to find him rehab," I said.

In front of us, a dragon twisted out of the sand, stretches of his tail buffed smooth by the wind. Next to him, a life-size replica of the *Pietà* eroded at an angle. Mary made of sand gazed down at her dead son; her face disappeared from the chin up, like a dune. But her eyes were still there, full of love and fear. Maybe all memories of home were like this—eroding, mineral, made of sea air.

"You kidding me? He's never going to quit. Not 'til he's dead." His voice floated across the wind, and his accent moored his words like anchors. "Are you going to Colorado for Christmas?"

Phil was talking about Frank smoking heroin in the garage, with the kids in the house. He was also talking about his long-dead baby brother, Dennis. My dad knew a thing or two about addicts.

"Dad. Maybe he'll get help. Come on," I said. "But I can't get all caught up in everyone else's problems all the time. I think I'm going to stay in New York for Christmas."

My pops and I looked back over the whole of the beach of our lives, and the lives of everyone we know, because some worlds are very small.

"Okay. Maybe people can change, Nicole. What do I know? I'm just an old man."

ANYTHING TO GET CLEAN

*My mom (l), Christine, and her friend, my aunt Debbie (r),
at a bar in Boston in the mid-1990s*

A few weeks after I returned from Boston, a cab dropped me off on the corner of 110th Street, across the street from my building. The gingko trees lining the wide sidewalks of Central Park North exploded in bright yellows. Black and lacquered streetlamps dotted the park, designed to resemble the gas lanterns of the Olmsted days.

I was home between teaching creative writing classes to clean my apartment before the new guests arrived for the week, two girls in their twenties from Milan.

I told my dad about the money Airbnb brought in because that part made us both happy. But I hadn't told him the work it entailed. Nothing came easy, especially not honest money. I scrubbed the toilet to find my new freedom.

Phil was so psyched about the *para*, I didn't want to ruin it for him. He told everyone I was a professor at NYU, even though I was an adjunct lecturer at City College. It didn't matter that I'd told him and told him; he heard what he wanted to hear. By his estimation, I was the most brilliant scholar on earth. Sure. I let us both have it. It felt nice.

I enjoyed the visit with my father. Gloucester was warm with nostalgia and late-summer sun, but going home felt empty.

The surprise of that emptiness made me miss my tiny, full life in New York.

Once inside the building, I willed the elevator to arrive faster. I smashed "up" over and over and heard it rumble into action on six. The elevator always stopped a half foot below the floor and sometimes in between floors, exposing the building's thick concrete supports.

My building's wide foyer recalled a splendor that Harlem hadn't seen since the turn of the twentieth century, when Manhattan's elite headed uptown for weekend and summer getaways. An intricate, tiled mosaic covered the lobby floor, interrupted by round columns with angels in the crown molding, painted green and gold. They held up the heavens and the ceiling. Glamorous stuff. In the foyer, you could hoot and hear its return up on six. You live *here?* friends often asked me.

The apartments that faced the park were either three or six bedrooms. They were enormous, with two bathrooms, a dining room, *and* a living room. A whole house. The back of each floor had small apartments that faced 111th Street—two bedrooms, a shoebox living room, a three-foot kitchen, and a bathroom to match. These had been for the cooks, cleaners, and au pairs of the grand apartments across the hall. The maids' quarters. That was where I lived.

Renting out my house meant I told visitors the same things over and over—the way the key stuck in the lock, or how the shower grout never got *clean* clean, or not to open their window because the AC wasn't screwed in. Several European guests had expressed disappointment that their church service hadn't had choirs, so I added the churches that did to the neighborhood binder.

Importantly, I told them if anyone asked, they were to say they were visiting their old friend Nicole. My lease stipulated I couldn't rent for a term shorter than thirty days, but the rent kept going up and up, and I wanted to stay in my apartment. That Harlem and its churches were featured in travel sites and guidebooks was a symptom of its gentrification. The fact that I could charge $150 a night on weekends was a bittersweet deal at best. The building owners wanted me out. I didn't like that. And the owners didn't like the idea of tenants making money they could be making. The popularity of Airbnb meant tourists were way up, and way visible. Everyone was on edge.

Airbnb sent over a professional photographer who used natural sunlight and wide angles to maximize my "cozy" space and made the apartment and the website look more appealing. Within days of going live, my second bedroom was booked six months into 2016. The immediate influx of money from the room provided relief from the anxiety of renting it.

The money also meant I could stop the constant addition and subtraction of direct deposits and bills and nights out and new shoes that had occupied a not-insignificant portion of my energy since my first job when I was fourteen. I never had enough. I always had to wait and see and let the charges clear.

Before Airbnb, I waited tables and bartended at Pangea, a fixture of the East Village that catered to an aging crowd of gay artists on fixed incomes. They were wonderful. But some nights I made less than $100 in tips, and some brunches I only made my $30 shift pay. Sometimes Pangea couldn't pay my shift pay until their rent cleared. I worked and waited for my student loans to come in. I searched for roommates on Craigslist and took creative writing master's classes at City College, on its grand campus on Convent Avenue where I would go on to adjunct. I paid the rent on the slip that slid under the door every month and built my home out of street finds and hand-me-downs. I loved my apartment in that way that attends the possession of that which you'd only dreamed of, which is to say, unhealthily.

Those first few years in New York, I dragged bookshelves and broken couches down avenues like corpses. I swapped price tags on wall art at Anthropologie and stole cashmere throws from Marshalls. I inherited furniture and bookshelves from fancier friends moving to cheaper liberal cities like Austin or Portland (either Portland). Begging, borrowing, and stealing were the only ways I knew how to build a life, but I did build.

I was lucky to have a big courtyard, and my apartment got excellent light. The building opposite ours was painted bright white, and its magnified light filled my apartment. My building's steam vent reflected against its white wall, and I often watched the steam's shadow pour out, crisp and frantic in the sunshine, endless.

Before I left new guests alone, we practiced opening the door together. I stood inside the apartment and yelled at them to turn the key past where they thought they should—turn it until they thought it might break.

"More! More!" I shouted.

When the door sprang open, we were reunited, smiling, in on it together.

The living room had two long windows and a soft-yellow corduroy couch I'd bought like new from a woman in Bay Ridge. The inherited bookshelves and the mid-century chair sat against the far wall. There were two coffee cups in the kitchen sink, which was no larger than a mixing bowl.

I had lived my entire life around strangers, so this arrangement didn't pose a problem for me. My mom and stepdad, Mike, moved Lindsay and me, then my younger siblings, Chelsea and Michael, so much with the military. I started a new school in a new state with new friends as often as every few months. It was disorienting to grow up on the move, and exhausting. I always wanted to stay. As an adult, I liked to keep a couple mugs on me, a relic of my childhood need to measure my security. It made me feel like I had a home.

My family prided ourselves on traveling light. Endless cycles of packing and unpacking made our possessions something we thought about intensely for a moment and then not again for weeks, months, or sometimes years. By then, little inside seemed essential anymore.

In the sink was one such mug—essential—that I bought in 2003, on a rainy trip to Boston. It was from the Rembrandt exhibit at Boston's Museum of Fine Arts and featured the etching *Self-Portrait in a Cap, Open-Mouthed*, from 1630. Rembrandt is wearing a floppy beret and looking over his shoulder, lips pursed. He looked young and silly. I loved going to the museums in Boston. They were a beautiful escape, and only my mom's eccentric friend Debbie ever wanted to go with me. She lived in the West Village when I was a kid, and visiting her was my first memory of New York.

We watched the early years of the Gay Pride March down Christopher Street from Auntie Debbie's apartment window, joy and anger at the height of the AIDS epidemic. We spent sweaty summer days in Chinatown, where my mom clamped down on our little wrists and said, "Come on, girls, let's go." And go we did. We bought brass and ivory jewelry from the street vendors up and down Canal Street; we bought books from the Strand, with its levels and levels of books unimaginable to a little girl who loved books. We devoured the pastries with burnt sugar bottoms that Debbie brought home from the famous bakery where she worked. I can't remember the name of the place and Debbie died not too long ago, so I can't ask her anymore. She was the last of her siblings, none of them very old. She'd said the prescription drugs and compound tragedies would finish every last one of them, and she wasn't wrong.

The Rembrandt mug in the sink in Harlem reminded me of Debbie and home. I washed it quickly and set it on the little Ikea rack that hung above the sink to dry. The stove had a few crumbs between the burners, and I wiped it down and swept the floors. The French girl had rinsed the French press, and I dried it and put it on the counter next to the coffee.

In the bathroom, the light lit the pubes and head hairs resting on the little puddles left behind after pre-airport showers. A soapy ring ran around the tub, the result of impressive water pressure and a not-so-impressive drain.

The bathroom was where I spent most of my time explaining a one-hundred-year-old building to my guests—American guests, that is. Visiting from the wide swath of the American suburbs, shining and shallow, my American guests sucked their teeth at the leaky windows. They scrubbed the grout in vain and questioned my use of scented detergent. I swear to God, Americans are the only people on this earth who can destroy the charm of a prewar. Every other visitor came from somewhere much older. When I showed them the shower or the sticky door, they did the *ppppth* or *euh* or whichever clicky sound of dismissal was native to whichever country they came from. Eventually I stopped booking Americans, if I could avoid it.

I honed my hustle to the point that running a hotel out of my apartment seemed *reasonable*. I learned that succeeding in New York relied on a lesson Boston taught me well: run and run and don't stop.

BEFORE I MOVED TO NEW YORK, my childhood friend Ashlie and I stood on her porch in Denver. Whenever the wind picked up, her begonias shed petals that shuttled across the lawn.

"You think you're going to save the world?" she asked, not looking at me.

"I need to save myself," I said. And it was true.

I needed to save my life from my family, immediate and extended. Every last one of them wanted and wanted, filled up with need. The problem was that I was filled with need, too, and I couldn't meet theirs at the expense of my own anymore. I was almost thirty, and the oldest daughter of a Navy *and* Marine, Catholic *and* Orthodox, Italian *and* Albanian family. My job was to serve others before serving myself. Moving to New York was the first time I prioritized my future, and not that of my parents' or younger siblings'. I wanted to fall in love and write books, so I moved to the best place to do both. I knew Manhattan because Debbie had lived there, and I thought if she could, I could too.

Debbie once told me that when she went skydiving and

the plane reached altitude, she couldn't jump. She came back down, unchanged. I decided I would always jump.

Living in New York City felt like a great leap, like falling into a new horizon. I learned best by making mistakes until I got it right, and it was a place where persistence was rewarded. I said or did the wrong thing all the time. Too loud and in the wrong place, that's me. But I turned up and I learned. I gathered the crumbs I could use to survive, and I was nice to people. I have a booming laugh that makes me a henball, like the rest of my family. I made friends easily, a real neighborhood girl. I fit right in to New York, a town that loved a fun fuckup willing to try.

All that hustle made me a great host. I went to the spare bedroom and stripped the bed and gathered the sheets and towels and brought everything to the laundry room in the basement. I kept a porcelain head full of quarters in the living room and was usually the only person in the bank who was stacking rolls. I did the laundry and the cleaning myself to keep turnaround high and my costs low. The timing of the laundry service didn't match my schedule, and I didn't want to spend the money.

I pulled the corners off the fitted sheet and it popped into the center of the bed. The scent of a stranger rose to meet me. I made a mental note to update my listing to indicate guests should strip their own sheets. Their smell was worse than their pubes in my opinion. I didn't want to know them like that. I wanted them gone.

One of the things I liked about Airbnb was that I never had to live with any one person for longer than a few weeks. The trade-off was living with hundreds of people a year. But at three to ten days a pop, I barely saw my guests, let alone got to know anyone beyond saying hello. Though the apartment was smaller than most imagined, the bedrooms were on opposite ends, which provided a merciful few feet of privacy. I could shut the door against the hotel of my home.

I had two hours between classes. The laundry cycle took ninety minutes on a tight schedule, and then a ten-minute cab ride back to campus. I started the wash and figured if I moved efficiently, I would race up the broken escalators at City College and arrive three minutes before my class started.

While the sheets swished around in the hot water, I sat down to check my phone. A new Tinder message appeared from a Turkish visiting professor.

In addition to finding roommates online, I found my partners and lovers on the various dating apps as well. I dated beardy, bespectacled, striped-socked overgrown boys in hoodies and beanies; captains of media, law, diplomacy, and the academy. I wanted their smarts and success to say something about my own.

And if I'm being as generous as possible to the men I gave it up to against whichever wrought iron fence in whichever neighborhood—theirs, mine, or Alphabet City—I forgave them. I forgave them because I could admit I was a real mark when it came to the affairs of the heart. I wanted to be loved so badly and to be seen as exceptional. I confused men's attention for confirmation of my worth; their charm and success for love and goodness. And I cried in a lot of taxis and elevators when none of that turned out to be true. Curled up in my bed, bleeding and bruised, I wondered, *Is this what love is supposed to feel like?*

But I didn't know. I don't know that any of us knew. We played on a field we built as we went along. One of my friends kept a dating spreadsheet, with weighted columns for things like "passion," "success," and "hair." (Primo usage of a spreadsheet, if you ask me.) She dated a perfect 100, once, and she didn't even like him that much.

So I forgave them their half-hard dicks and bad excuses and I started anew. Seeing that I worked for CUNY, the Turk said he did too. He asked what I taught and if I wanted to meet up that Saturday night, Halloween. I looked at his pictures again, then closed Tinder. His message arrived that morning. I wanted to wait before I responded.

RETURNING TO THE KITCHEN, I moved fast. After ten minutes, I had wiped down the surfaces and handles with hot soapy water and a clean water rinse. I scrubbed the kitchen floor on my hands and knees, which seemed impressive but became less so considering there were only twelve tiles. My mother taught me to put down a dish towel and give my knees grace. She said to start at the top and scrub your way back, so you have an exit in mind.

With twenty minutes before the wash finished, I had enough time to clean the bathroom. It took ten minutes, but I needed a break from the chemical cloud that accumulated, even with the October air in the open window. I hated the bathroom. The floor was always wet, and the scum stain never came clean. Sweeping the bathroom turned the broom bristles matted and wet. I balanced one foot on the sink and pivoted from my hip to obtain the optimal body angle to scrub the tub, but it didn't make a difference. No matter the acrobatics or the scrubbing bubbles, it remained a grout-stained, scummy tub.

A granddaughter of the Adriatic, a cleaning lady in bleachy ecstasy, I got dizzy scrubbing, my arms high and waving. The domestic instructions and proportions came natural like little else. I could get the scuff marks off a white sneaker. I could free a stain.

It wasn't something I did solely for the lodgers who paid my rent. I soothed with scrubbing and sweeping. I felt my best when the space sparkled. Creating order out of chaos provided me with agency. My sister, Lindsay, did laundry. Moving clothes from the dirty pile to the clean pile felt like power to her. She rarely folded the clothes, and sometimes the piles slid into one another and got washed again. I imagined in the year since she found Frank high, she shoveled everything in, trying anything to get clean.

I checked the timer on my phone. Forty-five seconds before the washing machine buzzed. I flipped the deadbolt on the front door so it didn't swing shut and autolock. I pushed the down button repeatedly until the elevator groaned into action.

The lights never worked in the basement, and there were locked rooms full of dead tenants' antiques and crimes. The *Project Runway* lady who lived on four only did her laundry in the middle of the night to avoid crowds, something I loved and feared about her.

I gathered the dryer-warmed sheets to my chest and went back upstairs, where I found my monthly rental slip face down in the living room. I flipped it over, wishing I could leave it unread.

I put the slip on the desk in my bedroom and saw I missed a call from my dad, along with three texts and a voicemail. I sat on my windowsill to smoke a bowl. I went through a fifty-dollar bag of weed a week, which in New York was a pitiful amount for the price. I tried to restrain myself for budgeting and productivity purposes, but getting high was the only way I managed my anxiety, so I always failed.

After spending time with my family, it took me a few weeks to recuperate. And here was Phil, planning another visit.

I lay down on my bed and put my phone on speaker, the volume turned down to nearly nothing.

"Ya, Nicole," my dad's voice boomed. He was half-deaf now and wouldn't get a hearing aid due to vanity and general opposition to the VA. He called from somewhere on St. Pete's Beach, where he bounced around short-term rentals since leaving his broke-down mobile home on Treasure Island.

"It's your *fatha*. Listen, I don't want you to worry, okay, but I need you to do me a *fay-vah*. I can't get my laptop fixed until I get my check next week, and then I gotta take it to the guys at Best Buy or something. I don't know what to do. Can you fucking believe it? Viruses? The luck?"

In the advanced Internet year of 2015, why was Phil's laptop full of viruses? Porn, I guessed. Or gambling, or some combination. I hated that I knew this, but I hated more the way the truth took a moment to make a dummy of me. I always believed him. His voicemail continued.

"So, listen, I want you to use your computer and look up plane tickets from Tampa to New York, okay? I know you're *busy.* I know you think I'm an adult and I can do it *myself,* but you gotta help your old man out. I'll give you my credit card number and you can punch it in for me. No big deal. Gimme a call back, all right? Love you. Gooooooo Pats."

I got up to put the clean sheets on the guest bed. I swept and placed the folded towels on the bottom right corner. *Why can't he be like everyone else's dad? How am I supposed to live my life and live his too? Can't he find a girlfriend?* I arranged the guest book and the basket of neighborhood guides, tours, and take-out menus on the dresser in the guest room.

With my purse and tote and denim jacket in my arms, I left the apartment and placed the extra keys under my welcome mat. I took the stairs that spiraled five flights in impressive marble. I held the banister tight and spun down fast, ever braced for impact.

I'd call my father after class. Then I'd make a date with the Turkish professor for Halloween.

THE CYBORG AND THE TREE

A friend outside of KGB Bar, East Village, New York City

For our first date, the Turk suggested we meet at a bar off Bleecker Street. I arrived and found him waving from within a crowd of NYU undergraduates in costume. He was tall with glasses, a beard, and shaggy dark hair, easy handsome. He smiled like he was happy to see me too. I made my way to him. He apologized in his thick accent and said he'd only lived in the city a month, so he picked a bar near the trains. We ordered beers and sat knee to knee, trying to talk over the din of a Halloween party in full swing. We were a stillness in a sea of drunk movement, young ghouls and pretty girls spinning past us. Before the next drink, he asked if I wanted to go somewhere we could talk.

"I know the perfect place," I said.

We walked across town to the East Village, almost touching in the cool night. We passed under the KGB BAR neon sign on Fourth Street and climbed the front stairs. Inside, another steep flight up to the dark red room on the second floor. The bar had black tables and long windows that looked out onto the street, but you'd never know—the red velvet drapes were always drawn. Russian propaganda posters, little candles, and enormous mirrors filled the room. "Communist chic," they called it.

When I worked at Pangea, a few blocks north on Second Avenue, our night shifts often turned into early mornings at KGB. We crammed into the tiny bathroom stalls and snorted coke with strangers until the sun came up. We laughed or cried together on the floor. I loved KGB.

The Turk loved it too. Of course he did. He was a communist, he told me over beers. We sat at a banquette along the wall and he explained his PhD in game theory, his visiting professorship, and the life in Turkey he left behind. He described the video game he was building, a game meant to teach political history and theory to its players. He told me he wanted to be a cyborg.

Surely, this was a bit. I smiled. "You want to be a cyborg?"

"Yes. I want to obliterate the attachments that make us feel and suffer. I want to be alone with my thoughts and my cigarettes. Like a cyborg. Or an astronaut."

I couldn't understand. I wanted to feel and suffer. The loneliness of space scared me. Looking back, this should've been a moment to realize what kind of people we were. What we could or couldn't give each other.

But, god. He was tall and handsome and political and passionate. How could a cyborg floating in space be close enough to admire me, a tree, whose branches and leaves rustled with anxious energy? Not knowing the answers, I decided the incongruity meant we contained multitudes.

The Turk went to the bar. "I have no idea what this guy is talking about," I texted my best friend, Casey. "His thighs are incredible. I want to make out with him forever."

Before he returned, Casey texted a screenshot of his profile page at the college.

"Got him. Carry on," she said.

Casey ID'd every potential date's social media profiles, workplaces, and exes before she met them. This was a service she extended to her friends as well. A font of information and tactics, Casey was the friend who made sure no potential Tinder murder went unsolved. The Turk placed the fresh beers on the table and sat down. I slid closer to him, secure I'd be avenged. His faculty picture was cute.

After a few beers, we went outside to smoke and made out on KGB's stoop. And it really did feel like forever. People hummed in a river behind us. They smoked their cigarettes; they arrived and left the bar. He took off my glasses and kissed my eyelids, holding my face in his hands. When he put them back on, they fogged. He asked me to go home with him, and because I liked him, I said no. I don't remember how I got home or when we left each other. When I think of that night I think only of his hands on my face, his lips on my eyes.

The next night I met my friend Tracy for drinks on the Upper West Side. Tracy's family was from Boston and she was a writer too. We were outrageous—born to be friends. The appetite on her, my god. Over several plates of chicken wings, I told her about the Turk, our first date, and the consequent eyelid-kissing situation.

"Treska, he kissed your eyelids and you didn't go home with him?" Her own eyes wide with surprise. "Are you okay?"

It was crazy, I knew it. His move was unprecedented. It did not appear on any spreadsheet I'd seen. The Turk arrived, a dispatch from some romantic land. I had never been treated with such reverence, and it left me discombobulated. I was listening to "Crazy for You" by Madonna, on loop. "Hounds of Love" by Kate Bush. I had it bad.

"I don't think I'm okay," I said. "I really don't."

For our second date, the Turk asked to cook me dinner and I said yes.

I went to his apartment in Sunnyside, Queens. He cooked kofte, Turkish meatballs, and played Animal Collective. He said he googled "cool music" for me. And he said that his oven was big enough to make kofte for a Kurdish army. The apartment was big, Queens big, and empty save a couch, a bookshelf, and a table against the window. A single Turkish soccer scarf hung on the wall. Over dinner he told me how he and other protesters had occupied Camp Armen, an Armenian orphanage under threat of destruction. The protestors lived there for months and won it back from the government.

He teared up when he told me he wanted his grandfather to know freedom again before he died. I thought he was like Marius from *Les Misérables*—a revolutionary with a poet's heart—which is to say, I fell in love with him over kofte.

Afterward, we sat on the couch and drank wine from yogurt jars. Between dates, he'd emailed me "A Cyborg Manifesto" by Donna J. Haraway, and I spent the intervening week reading the essay.

I told him I liked that Haraway saw a cyborg's rejection of the family unit as a possible answer to the oppressions of the patriarchy. I liked that the cyborg's disloyalty signaled hope and that its existence represented dangerous possibilities. Freedom. At the same time, much of the essay eluded me. I enjoyed theory, but it wasn't my preference. It always left me reaching for its meaning.

"I guess I prefer literature to teach me. It's easier for me to understand those big ideas through narrative."

"Yes, because stories are easy. Theory teaches you the tools to build and dismantle ideas, empires. It's harder because it's more important."

"I don't think one's better than the other. You're taking the lid off the maze and analyzing from above. You know the language. You label the systems. I am in the maze, rendering it for the next person. That's important too. A map changes things."

I was reaching for the Turk, translating right from the beginning.

I told him about Lindsay's panicked calls to me. I told him about her missing money and Frank's glassy eyes. I didn't want to go to Denver; I felt both protected and alienated by the distance I put between me and my family.

He smiled, his nicotine-stained teeth crooked and perfect.

"See? You could be an astronaut," he said. He leaned up and over me, his arms long, his biceps nice.

"Do you *vant* me?"

I said yes, yes, yes and slid between his thighs to swallow him whole before we fucked on the couch.

The next morning on the train back to Harlem, I googled "Turkey" and "PKK" and "Kurdish territories," my heart and mind and body throbbing with want for the new.

CATFISHED

Phil and me, 110th Street, New York City, November 2015

Phil arrived for his birthday the week after I met the Turk. His birthday was November 11, Veterans Day. A big deal for a man whose military service served as a pillar of his personhood. He showed up with his shirt unbuttoned far below the respectability line and his Albanian wool tufting up over the buttons. His knee seemed more sideways than usual. Even with his bullet dodger's strut, I could tell he was limping. He took the bus from LaGuardia and got off at 110th Street and Broadway, a half mile from my apartment on Central Park West. He walked down the hill, stopping to swear every block. He preferred agony to a ten-dollar cab ride, my old man.

When Phil visited me in Harlem, it was evident he was a sidewalk savant, a corner store natural. His first order of business was to walk slowly to whichever deli was nearby and post up. He asked questions about the griddle, business. Fluent. He came home with Boar's Head ham and American cheese wrapped first in paper, then in foil. He told me about the old-timer he met on the corner.

"I was walking home, and we got to talking. He's a vet too!" my father said. "So I bought him a coffee."

By the end of his trips, Phil met everybody.

"Phil!" they called from the streets. He shouted back and threw a hand up in salutation, dipped his shoulder to make it personal. "Eh, my guy!"

"You know Roy?" I asked, waving at my neighbor. Roy was a retired boxer who lived in the building next door. He hung out on the stoop and watched the traffic to and from the trains. Roy walked with a tilt too. He was also a neighborhood guy.

"Roy was pro!" my dad says. "I told him how I used to box, down at the Y on Huntington Avenue. And Papa too. I was good before I went to war!"

PHIL ENLISTED IN THE MARINES in 1967, after a fight in Somerville at Davis Square. He won the fight when he put the kid through a glass pastry case. A Boston devastation if ever there was one.

Drunk in the cruiser, Phil called the cops whores. He told them to fuck themselves and cursed at them in Albanian. Phil laughed while they booked him, and then they beat him in his cell, seven cops deep. It took three months to unwire his jaw. When it happened, days after his eighteenth birthday, he walked into the Marines' enlistment office and swapped out one fight for another.

So, there's Phil. Just a kid. Eighteen years old in the DMZ (demilitarized zone) in 1968. He sat on a V-boat into his first firefight in Vietnam, cocky and popping off his mouth.

The way he told it—and he told it a lot, this myth of becoming—Phil was on his first operation and a commanding officer stopped to listen to him pontificate. The CO was one of those head-made-of-rock guys with boulder biceps. Stone-faced. He placed his hands on his knees and bent down as he said to Phil, "We'll see if you're talking this big when you get back. If you get back."

Phil hadn't considered the second clause. Dead. The boat went too fast, and the wake split the river. The next time they met was in the Tet Offensive. Phil didn't know if that CO made it out or got mowed down by one of his own. He said one minute it was quiet, the next, tracers skipped past his head and lit the night. All hell opened up, he said. Everyone around him either died or disappeared—Do you know what they did?—until it was only Phil and the war.

He left Vietnam after two tours, a twenty-year-old man on a helicopter full of the dead and dying, his knee full of shrapnel. More were dead and dying in the jungle below. The *thwop-thwop* of the chopper echoed the beat of my father's very own heart. He came home. His battalion was awarded a presidential unit citation for being one of the most active combat battalions in Vietnam.

All of that fucked him up, heading into a war he didn't understand and heading out traumatized and disabled. The life he had planned for himself was blown to smithereens. He reassembled it, but it was never the same.

He had changed.

It was like Phil was still in Vietnam, and the smoke of the burning wouldn't leave him. The scars from the jungle rot stayed on him for thirty years. Lindsay, me, and his women, we woke up to his nightmares. We learned to sit with our backs to the door and on the inside of every booth, theater row, and kitchen table. My father was always on the outside, looking for the exit. We kept our eyes on him and on the door.

And he needed us. Phil liked to buy one-way plane tickets

and gas by the single gallon. He rinsed and reused McDonald's coffee cups until they disintegrated. His plates were empty cold-cut containers. He didn't own a fork. He showed up at my house every time with one pair of underwear. One pair.

MY FATHER WAS AS BAD at understanding the nuances of social media as he was with most other communication. He was unaware that when he posted on other people's pages or replied to their posts, what he wrote was visible to his friends. And over the past few months, his Facebook revealed more and more questionable behavior.

He posted a young woman's page every few days. *Wow!* he'd say with rose and heart-eye emojis. Her photo resembled a stock image from a catalog: busty and blonde surrounded by hay bales. She wore a red-and-white gingham shirt knotted between her breasts in a *Dukes of Hazzard* sort of way. She said she was from Montana. Outside of a series of recent "updates" from Kenya, her profile was empty. Her photos appeared in my feed when Phil commented on her beauty. My sister and I sent screen grabs of the old man's posts back and forth.

"He doesn't know we can see him, does he?"

He did not. And it wasn't like Lindsay needed the hassle. Her silences over the phone revealed more than she offered up about her life. She couldn't put words to it, so she let the long line drift to Phil and his antics.

"Don't let him send any more money, okay?" she said, exhausted. I promised I wouldn't.

The morning after Phil arrived, we walked to the café on the corner, and he handed me his old Nokia with a glowing green screen and buttons too tiny for fingers as thick and old as his.

"Can you tell me why I can't see my messages?"

"Dad, how do you even use this thing?"

The back was held on with masking tape and the screen flickered as it connected to the Internet. Facebook pulled up and the font looked analog. I clicked into his inbox and found several unread messages from the blonde.

"Philip, I thank you so much for your talk the other day. Your words were kindnesses."

And:

"My dear, what you've done is a blessing from God. We will thank you forever. I cannot wait to see you."

The language in the messages looped. The idioms felt beautiful in a way American sayings were not.

"I cannot wait for you in Tampa."

I put the phone down. Phil waited for an answer, making little "gimme" motions with his hand. He tried to see what I was doing.

I showed him the busty blonde and asked, "Who is this woman?"

"She's my friend. What? We send each other messages, that's it!"

"You know, Lindsay and I have been talking about this for weeks."

"You can see what I post?!"

His eyes went big as dollar coins on a dead man, the way they always do when you tell him something shocking, like men didn't pay for dinner on dates anymore, or hotel rooms cost more than $100 a night. It was charming. It was a shakedown.

"Dad. Everyone can see everything you post. That isn't a private message. Who is this?"

"She got stuck in Kenya! She's been lonely for home, so we talk! It's nothing."

"Have you given her money?"

"I never gave her any money, c'mon, Nicole."

Swatting at me across the table, he grabbed his phone. I would never know how much money Phil gave the Facebook account. He would take that information to his grave, and we both knew it.

I asked him what they talked about, my seventy-year-old father and this twenty-some-year-old woman. How homesick was she, I wondered aloud, that she reached out across the vast ocean of time and space to talk to the one, the only, Phil Treska.

"You think I don't know her? I wake up to 'Hello, handsome,' and I go to sleep to 'Sweet dreams.' What else is there to know?"

"Having someone to talk to isn't the problem, Dad. I think you're getting catfished."

"There are no fish! What are you talking about? We're only talking!"

I told my father what *catfishing* meant and explained to him who was most susceptible and why. He was incredulous and confused. And then he demanded his phone back.

"Watch this," I said.

I navigated to his text messages and typed into the blinking bar, narrating as I went. "This is Nicole, Phil's daughter. Stop texting my father. I'm calling the police."

Phil lurched backward like he'd been shot.

"Nicole, the police? What are you doing to my life?"

"Look, I love love. I want love. I want you to have love. But I won't let you get taken for a ride."

74

The Turk had told me he couldn't be anyone's boyfriend. Three weeks before we met, his long-distance girlfriend of seven years broke up with him. He came to New York to be with her and found her in another relationship. She walked him to a home goods store and helped him buy a spatula. Then she left.

He wanted to see me when he wanted to, he said, and he'd made that clear from the beginning. I figured he gave what he had to the people, not to a single person. I loved him and admired him, so I viewed his absences as heroic and magnanimous. When he came and came again, the way our bodies moved together, our time together—I took it to mean something true. Most of my life, I'd yearned for the men I wanted to want me back, and to have that yearning met and matched felt so powerful. I was sure it must be love.

"I love being with you and talking with you. I could talk to you all day. But I can't give you what you want," the Turk told me.

Both my father and I turned a blind eye to the truth to hold on to what we thought we loved. We saw what we needed to see.

I spent so much of my life trying not to date my father, it surprised me to realize how much I was *of* my father. I looked at him there, miserable. My want to protect him was, in part, a want to protect myself.

"Listen, Nicole," my father said, "I'm nobody's fool, okay."

I smiled. "Please, take my advice. I'm not using it."

His phone chimed.

I love your kind and romantic father. Why do you speak of police?

Incredulous, I read the text aloud to my father while typing a response.

Which town in Montana are you from, exactly? Which church sent you on mission? How much money has he sent you?

I asked my father the last question as well. I was angry. Phil watched my face for an indication he was in as much trouble as he thought. He was sheepish.

"What, Nicole? I had a lot on my mind. She kept me company."

"Your phone is mine now. I'm telling them I'm calling the police. We'll report the Facebook account, but I'm sure there's no way to track these people."

My father worked through the idea of various hands far away, various voices sending him lullabies.

"People?" I saw his shame and its sudden devastation.

I couldn't be angry that my father was so lonely he'd been taken advantage of because I told myself lies to keep from feeling lonely too. But I couldn't live with him realizing he'd been played for a fool. I tried to deflect the weight we were feeling, but the horrors of being alive and vulnerable hit us both like a locomotive.

"Listen, this happens all the time. That's why there's a name for it. The Internet makes it so easy to connect with people, and you're a trusting person, so of course you thought that she was real. Of course you thought this person was telling you the truth!"

He was nodding now, my father. He was happy to hear this information but still not convinced.

"But how come you knew right away? How do you know and I don't? How do you know she's not who she says she is?"

I told him I lived online, and I had since I was a kid. I was fluent and interpreting for him. But there was always a feeling of inadequacy with translation—of reaching. Something left on the table, and it was all over Phil's face.

He squeezed my hand with his needful affection. That same affection used to irritate me. Now, I applied it to those I loved.

"I believe you. Am I a stupid guy for being lonely?"

I filled with tears. My father, old and duped, was close to tears too.

"No, Pops. You're not stupid. You've got a big heart, and big hearts do dumb things. I'm a dummy for love too."

An interesting thing happened in my twenties. I set a lot of boundaries around what I did for my father. He wasn't, for example, allowed to purchase airplane tickets without checking with me. He couldn't stay longer than two weeks. He needed a return ticket when he arrived.

I set firm stakes, born as I was to tell him I was his daughter and not his servant. I refused to call the airlines or make his reservations for him. Over his *whole* life, women tended to his every need and I was sick of being pushed around by his helplessness.

"You have all the time in the world," I said. "I'm too young to take care of you."

The difficulty of enforcement turned into a war I always lost—one that ended with punching credit card numbers into my laptop, both of us angry and tired.

But into my thirties, I was beginning to realize it wasn't that my father wouldn't do these things for himself; it was that he couldn't anymore. The helplessness he'd felt or feigned his whole life was actual with age, and we could both feel it.

Fine.

I would buy the tickets. I would explain the way social

media worked, over and over again. I would wake up early to fix the coffee and do the best I could do to keep my dad from feeling far from power.

When it came to Phil, I was a hurricane. I generated electricity. Anger, love, and frustration swirled; I picked up speed. I looked at him across the table, and I saw his feelings churning too. His storm was made up of different fronts than mine, but it raged just the same.

"Hey." I put his phone face down on the table between us. "I know you don't want to believe me and you don't have to, but can you trust me?"

"Yeah, Kiddo. I can trust you. You're the smartest person I know."

As we walked home, the sun sparked through the trees on the north face of Central Park, and the shimmer danced off the buildings. It was a tree-lined, beautiful block with old brick facades where peregrine falcons and raccoons found places to perch. My dad's knee made it imperative that we moved slowly, but it was nice to enjoy the late-fall brightness.

I thought about the way poor families, Balkan and Mediterranean families—immigrant families—were built like this. For daughters to tend to their fathers, their husbands, their families, and then their fathers again. I rejected all that in the name of myself, and it felt radical and good. Yet in moments like this, the Hydra came for me, its tendrils powerful and long. No matter how far I ran.

He stopped on the sidewalk and leaned against the wall of the building next to mine.

"I can't help but thinking: what if she's out there and thinks I left her alone?"

RUN, BABY, RUN

The year I went to six first grades, Corpus Christi, Texas, 1985

That December, our building was sold to new owners. They wasted no time harassing tenants and driving out rent-stabilized and below-market renters. One morning before I left for work, the new superintendent shoved a thick manila envelope under my door. The rent slip typically came on carbon paper with perforated edges and a return envelope attached. It slid across the floor like an airboat before feathering out. This one was wedged under the door, ominously fat.

By the end of 2015, Harlem rents rose to meet the rest of Manhattan and Brooklyn. Most market-rate apartments in the neighborhood were going for well above $2,000, a staggering increase from only a few years before. Landlords knew that if they renovated a vacant, rent-stabilized apartment (replaced the cabinets and refrigerator, gave it a fresh coat of paint), they could list it as a luxury unit and charge twice the rent, thus pricing it out of stabilization.

Controlled demolitions exploded across Harlem. Skyscrapers replaced gas stations, churches, and mosques. Abandoned buildings dropped one by one.

The new owners installed cameras on every floor, and their lawyers combed tenant leases for what they claimed were exploited loopholes or illegal lease transfers. They leveraged anything they could leverage. The building bled tenants. Families that had raised their families and their families' family there—evicted. New building supers arrived, each more aggressive than the last. They showed up unannounced and pounded on our doors with closed fists, like the cops.

Anticipating that any infraction would be grounds to get rid of me, I adjusted my Airbnb operation. I'd been booking guests anywhere from a few nights to a few weeks, but now I only booked for longer than the thirty days stipulated in my lease. I removed any mention of my building or street address on my listing and took my photo off my profile. I operated within the rules, but I still didn't trust these supers, with their cameras and their thick envelopes getting pushed around all over the place. A tenants' rights organization held several meetings in the lobby of our building to address landlord intimidation, and I reached out to them for legal advice.

The Turk and I were seeing each other a few times a week at the end of 2015. I went to his airy, empty apartment and we ate and fucked and talked politics. He said to me, "Again?" and I nodded yes. I slept and he stayed up all night in the glow of his computer. He climbed into bed hard for me in the morning. We showered together and made little jokes in the streaming water. Then he kissed me good-bye and slept for eight hours. But even as our tangled bodies grew more familiar and the dates stacked up, he promised me he wasn't my boyfriend.

I reasoned that his absences were work related. He was a visiting professor who taught for a celebrity professor in his department. I worked in academia, too, and I knew that didn't mean anything about one's busyness. But when we did meet, I told myself not to ask too many questions so I could enjoy love. My whole life I'd controlled my feelings to protect myself. Moving a lot made a girl strange and needful. I learned that sometimes keeping love meant keeping my mouth shut. *Don't whisper your heart to anyone, Nicole.*

And not for nothing—when my mother was a child, she sat on the porch waiting for her father to trip his way home from the pub around the corner. The rare times he arrived with a toy piano or a picture book lit up her whole life. She still talked about those visits. I don't mean to say that the Turk owed me what my grandfather owed my mother, in attention or love, but I do mean to say I am my mother's daughter. And we, the daughters of women who loved men, we learned early to keep our big stupid mouths shut.

WHEN I WAS IN THE first grade, we lived in Corpus Christi, Texas, for less than six months. I played with bugs—roly-polies—in our sandy backyard, and in class I learned to draw the state of Texas, a strange and strangely shaped place I'd never been before. One day at lunch, I told a new friend I had a crush on Peter, Peter, Pumpkin Eater, the boy with shiny hair. And I saw her, this girl I had just met—in my memory, and what lives in our memory more than our greatest summers and our greatest humiliations?—I saw her turn to PPPE and whisper my heart to him down the lunch table. I spent the rest of my recesses at Flour Bluff Elementary School on the playground facing the wall, hiding my hurt. I'd already learned to wait it out. We wouldn't be there long. I went to six different first grades.

That same year we moved to Virginia, and my mom sat me on the edge of my bed to tell me my father would be going away to camp. What she didn't tell me, of course, was that Phil sold ounces of cocaine to an undercover agent at the post office, where he worked. He'd been arrested and found guilty and was going to prison. According to Phil, he was arrested for running books, and he only did it the one time; according to the *Boston Globe*, he was arrested for federal drug trafficking. My mother, years later, told me, "You were on a need-to-know basis, and you didn't need to know." I was six.

What did I know about camp? I knew summers at the park on Hancock Street putting beads in our hair and on safety pins and our sneakers and bike spokes so everything shook and clacked as we sped around the neighborhood. Camp meant four square and playing on tire swings and the ice cream truck and saying *fuck you* real loud without fear, like our parents did. It did not mean this somber thing happening on the edge of my Rainbow Brite bedspread. He'd be gone two years, my mom said.

She meant this to be a nothing chat, tailored to soothe my small worry and quell my endless questions, but it didn't. Two years of camp was like no camp I ever knew, and the confusion of that conversation was sewn forever into the stuff of my mind.

Lindsay and I spent the weekend with my dad before he went away. My mother, ever that little girl on the porch, knew how much it meant to have, or not have, a dad around, even a drug-dealing, deadbeat one. She always made sure we spent time with Phil despite his history of abuse and lack of child support.

That weekend, he did the thing where he cried so much. He told us how pathetic he was and that he'd be thinking of us at camp. Phil squeezed my hand and held me too hard into his side. He told me he'd always love me. My sister was too young for these talks and watched cartoons on the hotel TV. I watched her with envy.

My dad took us home that Sunday and stood on the walkway made of big, smooth stones my sister and I hopscotched across. He groveled a good-bye. I allowed myself to move closer to my father. I understood that he was going away and I wouldn't see him again for a long time; several weird chats clarified this information.

I still didn't get it. *I would kill to be at camp*, I thought, remembering my mom dropping us off at Hancock Street and watching us from the porch before going inside, assured we were safe.

THE TURK TOLD ME HE was conflicted about how much to see me, given his complicated heart. It hurt to hear him say what I suspected. Now I look at that hurt and that knowledge and I say: *run, baby, run*. I said it then too, but I couldn't follow through, because when he did reach out, I went to him. That lonely walk through the Times Square subway station, from the C train to the 7 train? From Manhattan to Queens? I did it. I did it every time he called. I knew that ride left me feeling queasy and unsure on my feet. But still, I went.

This was during the lead-up to the 2016 election, and the broad liberal swath, myself included, believed Clinton's success was imminent. The Turk was sure Trump would win.

During an early date, sprawled naked across each other on his couch, he asked me what kind of country I thought I lived in.

"What's that supposed to mean?" I asked.

"You live in Turkey too," he said. "You just don't know it yet. The mask will come off."

During this time, Turkey's president, Recep Tayyip Erdogan, increased violence and pressure on academics, leftists, Kurds, and anyone else who challenged his authority. The Turk left before most of his colleagues signed a letter of dissent, and now the state was arresting those academics and hauling them off to jail. Scared for his comrades, he wanted to return in solidarity. He saw the rising tide of right-wing violence lapping American shores and was certain of the election outcomes.

"But you told me Turkey is bombing Kurdish communities inside its own borders. It's dropping bombs on its own citizens. That can't happen here."

"Do you have any Black friends? Any Native American friends? Don't you know," he asked again, "what kind of country you live in?"

I polka-dotted my way across America my whole life and made friends everywhere, but I still had a naivete about America. About how it worked, and for whom. In some ways, I had a better sense of the country's samenesses and differences than most other Americans. But I was also the child of religious city folk in the military, and so in other ways, I'd grown up blinkered by their white, conservative lenses. In some ways, I didn't really know my country at all.

The Turk gawked when I said I saw progress belonging to Democrats and so believed that to be the party of progressivism.

"Liberals are on the left, too, right? So aren't they the same?" I asked, still unclear on the distinctions between a liberal and a leftist.

He walked out of the room, mumbling as I shouted *What?* after him.

While my definitions were not as clear as they would become, I did want progressivism and solutions to the devastation my family knew our whole lives, born of not having enough. The Turk gave me a new language for the ways I defined myself and my country and my desires for both. I kept that after he went away.

I also disagreed with him a lot and saw the ways his frameworks were flawed too. He had a healthy hatred for the police, which I shared, but I reminded him that the relationship between poor people and the cops was complicated. Many lower-income Americans saw a career in law enforcement or the military as a good life, one to be respected. Or at least a way out. The Turk's parents were academics. His mother was a translator and spoke seven languages. *Poor people* were theoretical to him. Our lives were theoretical to him. We argued over Hank in the TV show *Breaking Bad*, Walter White's cop brother-in-law who is played for a hero. I said Hank gave viewers a sense of hope. The Turk argued that whatever goodness Hank represented was spoiled by the fact that he was a police officer, thus inherently ungood. I said, I get it, I get it. But don't you get it? Uncle Stanley was a cop and a hero to the family. My cousins were cops, too, and had what was seen as an unimpeachably respectable gig.

I held many of the same opinions the Turk did, but I knew those opinions made me an outlier in my family. I knew no one wanted to hear my shit about how cops and mobsters weren't that different. I knew what they believed and why. It felt insane to me to pretend cops didn't come *from* the working class, even though I understood that cops didn't work *for* the working class. The Turk's position felt ideological, not lived. In moments like these, I found myself in the ways and the words of my parents: What good are your *booksmahts?*

CAT OUT OF THE BAG

*My uncle Dennis Treska, less than
a year before he died, Somerville, 1982*

I **decided to go** to Denver for Christmas. I was anxious about my heart and my home, and I needed distance from the Turk. After I arrived at my sister's he called to tell me he was going to Turkey. He didn't know for how long. Weeks, he said. I wondered if he waited until after I left to tell me. I wondered if his ex-girlfriend was going home too. I'd googled her. She looked a lot like me: bobbed, wavy hair somewhere between curly and frizzy, a round face with round features. She was smaller than me and dressed like an academic (you know, frumpy), but I could see it.

Like Phil, the Turk didn't have a return ticket. Like Phil, I fretted over it. *Why doesn't he know when he is coming back? Doesn't he care about me?* He was telling me this over a video call. I was quiet.

His face: handsome, bearded. He broke up as we spoke, his voice cutting out and bouncing off his bare walls. I broke up too, hearing what he said to me.

"I'll bring you back good tobacco."

I shoved my toe into the base of a small snowman my nephew, JJ, built in my sister's backyard.

"Yes. Bring me the contraband."

"Eh. Please don't use such words on these devices."

We laughed, but not much.

"I'll see you when I return."

At first, the doubt monster only emerged those rare times I watched the Turk sleep, even more handsome with all his tension released. Then it started to creep up my chest on the long train ride from his house to mine. After that, I saw the Turk leaving me everywhere. He was like the tortured man from *La Jetee*, Chris Marker's 1962 haunting sci-fi romance. The Turk came and went without warning, and I waited for him. I dreamed of his return. I wanted to believe that we would see each other when he came back, but I was beginning to doubt that too.

I went inside to escape the Colorado cold and locked the door of Lindsay's house. I moved from room to room, turning off the lights on the main floor. The front room was empty except for a pool table piled with bills and school projects and backpacks. Around the corner, a Christmas tree lit up the living room in a way we all needed, so I left it on.

I moved the laundry off the couch and onto the floor to make my bed. Upstairs, my niece and nephew were bunked up in JJ's room, and my mother stayed in Malia's room, painted with hot pink and black stripes. A sign on her door read: *Famley stay OUT!* She was seven going on eight, my niece, and already very smart.

Malia was four years older than JJ and conscripted into the role of caregiver for her brother. She was world-weary and frowned in a familiar way, a small adult. She loved her brother fiercely. I wished our family didn't keep making girls like us. Girls who bounced other people's babies on their knees, singing: *All the way to Boston, all the way to Lynn, watch out, little baby, that you don't fall in.*

WONDERLAND

While Phil was in Denver, he slept in the extra bedroom. Frank's daughter from his first marriage came over every other weekend, and when she arrived I moved to the smaller couch so Phil could stretch out on the long one. The dogs, two French mastiffs, slept wherever they wanted. Lindsay called them area rugs. They stretched underfoot, their big-dog dander floating through the air. The house rose and fell with the quiet of sleepful breathing from other rooms. The whole family together, trying to figure out love and home. And what did any of us know about love sticking around? Only what we'd learned by example: Don't hold your breath, and keep moving.

At Lindsay's, I could see for myself that Frank had moved from oxycodone to heroin. He was thin, and his eyes were glassed over like a cliché. His work as a house painter was seasonal. In the winter, when there was no work, he smoked cigarettes in the garage and played solitaire on his phone. During these cold, dry days, he dulled his edges with the pain pills he bought from his sister or stole from the houses he painted.

Acquiring pills became a problem that smoking heroin solved. And in those hours in the garage, alone and smoking, he spent all their money, borrowed more money, and spent that too. He went from a depressed guy to a depressed junkie and thief. Phil and my mother, thirty years divorced, moved in with Lindsay, Frank, and the kids. My sister Chelsea moved into the basement, after she got out of jail, and I came home to visit for Christmas. My brother, Michael, the youngest, only came over for dinner. He was smart too.

At that point, Frank was in and out of outpatient rehabs

and support groups. He went when the courts ordered him to go, but only then. He never committed to his own recovery as he sunk my sister and her children into debt. Suddenly my parents were paying most of her mortgage, cooking the meals, and watching the kids.

WE HAD LIVED IN DENVER after my stepdad, Mike, got out of the navy in 1993. He hoped to get hired by one of the major airlines setting up a hub out of Denver International Airport, but the job market dried up as soon as we arrived. My parents spent the next seven years in the suburbs, my longest home at the time, trying to pay for a middle-class life we couldn't afford. Daddy Mike, a pilot who flew enormous P-3 Orions for the navy, managed a Taco Bell in the civilian world. He tried to start his own landscaping company. At night, my mom wait-ressed or sold ceramics in homes around the neighborhood while Lindsay and I put the kids to bed. I got a job at a car wash when I was fourteen. I needed parental permission to work.

I went to high school in Littleton, a suburb twenty min-utes south of Denver. There, I learned about the middle class and honor rolls and minivans. Jansport backpacks and preppy clothes from the Gap dazzled me, but we could never afford the brand names and bought their rough approximations at Ross Dress for Less and Payless Shoes. It wasn't the same, and everyone knew it.

Where we roamed, Phil followed. He followed us to the shithole navy base towns we moved to, and the finer ones too. He stayed at the shithole hotel in the area, no matter where. He drove when he could drive and flew when he had to.

WONDERLAND

Phil hunted his children through the vast and strange country. He took us to Sizzlers and Olive Gardens and Burger Kings near his hotels. Regardless of time or place, our rituals in the homogeny of middle America created a sameness. That a rest stop could feel like some sort of home showed how adrift we were from what we knew. Burger King rest stops still make me say, *You know, we used to live in these.*

Our friends in Colorado visited us in hotels on the outskirts of town. They ran the patterned hallways, headed for the over-chlorinated pool. My friends lived in gated neighborhoods and had blonde, swingy, perfect ponytails (my frizzy and thin ponytail never stayed smooth). They watched Phil, broad shouldered and deeply tanned, wearing wet, white swim trunks, gesticulating while he asked them about what their *mutha*, their *fatha* did, giant and a little manic.

I knew who we were, and in those Colorado years, I learned who we weren't, and that it was something to be ashamed of. What these suburban kids saw, they saw without context. They didn't know what Italians were like, Albanians, or Bostonians. But it didn't matter; we lived in their town now. We were the different.

"They all talk like that," I said, to blunt the edge of their wonder. "It's not that big of a deal," I insisted with a shrug.

By the time I was a teenager, the years of McMansion developments and strip malls recurring, I had watched my friends gape at my family for years—at our generational jobs as servers, shift managers, used car salesmen. So I attempted to salvage something. Sure, Phil was funny.

My friends saw my family's time in and out of jail as suspect. Our annual income suspiciously low. Our accents suspiciously

95

broad. The way I paid for movies with dimes. The way my step-dad drove a Gremlin through a sea of brand-new Subarus. I took my friends home to Boston from time to time to show off the place I came from. *See? Do you see me?* I don't know if they did. I think they saw the guy pissing in the corner and the fight rolling out of the pub and into the street.

Denver never felt like home to me, but it was where my siblings found their home. And in this moment, Lindsay's house in the suburbs was overflowing with my family and our crises. It was an all-hands-on-deck shitshow, and that was as close to home as I'd ever known.

By the time I arrived in December, my mom and dad were roommates once again, and Phil and his grandson, JJ, were in deep camaraderie. Their closeness revolved around routine and chicken nuggets.

Every day, my dad picked JJ up from preschool. He parked my sister's SUV in the parking lot and got out with care from the great height. He lowered himself down on his good leg, and limped across the parking lot. JJ would be four soon and ran to his papa. He loved Phil.

Back in the SUV, Phil strapped the kid into his booster seat. JJ had autism, and Phil liked to say, "He's smarter than I'll ever be, I'll tell you that right now." JJ saw everything and computed. He listened and acknowledged net positive re-quests with stunning quickness, and ignored what didn't hold his attention. Seemed fair to me.

Lindsay had become an expert on the ways of his autism. She was a good mom and put years into dense paperwork and public school administration to determine the best ways for her son to learn. She hunted preschools and day cares to find a place that would work with him and his aides. After JJ was sent home from one, she cried in her truck: "They didn't even let him stay a week."

It was a struggle to get JJ into a good school, but once Lindsay found one, he blossomed. He asked questions and showed concern. He spoke in full sentences and made eye contact. He knew how to ask Phil for chicken nuggets from McDonald's, and he knew Phil knew the way to the drive-through.

Phil talked about his time in the house the way he talked about his time in Vietnam, and who were we to correct him? His life was defined by Boston, war, and fatherhood. Most other things, crime included, flowed from these. This act of giving in a way he didn't before was an act of valor, of service, and in that service, JJ was his closest brother-in-arms. His grandson. Same chin.

Lindsay ran an at-home day care until Frank's drug use put an end to that. She started working for the post office to pay the bills once things got bad. She worked hard. Lindsay worked hard at everything and loved her family. Suddenly, she found herself looking back in time, dealing with an addicted husband and working the same job Phil worked when we were babies.

In some ways, the post office job was perfect. City folk are civil servants deep down. If they keep their noses clean, they get a living wage and a pension. They didn't even have to like the job that much. Generations of civil servants or criminals, or both. That was us.

Lindsay was one of those kids who looked with disdain at the drug use and nefarious behavior of our entire family, appalled, like she was above us, or scared of us. Everyone thought Lindsay's lot would be mine—a junkie for a husband. Instead it was Lindsay, the athletic and beautiful. Lindsay, who moved mercurially into relationships that didn't work her whole life. But she made them work until they *looked* beautiful, and she could make them work for a long time. That was something she inherited from my mother. She made those relationships work into big yards with big dogs and beautiful babies, and she made her men more beautiful too. But she couldn't ever make them whole or make them do the right thing. And she couldn't bear it when they didn't.

In Denver, I found Lindsay's jaw taut and trembling. Her back rippled in a Treska way. I could see the recursions to previous iterations. The fighter. The desperate. The silent.

PHIL ARRIVED IN COLORADO TO be the father he'd always wanted to be, knowing he hadn't done so well the first time around. He paid Lindsay's mortgage for all the years of missing child support. Each month, Phil gave Lindsay large portions of his retirement and VA disability checks. He gave it to her because he loved her. An older, wiser Phil recognized the parallels between his own life and his daughter's. He saw the damage done and wanted to fix it, and he ached to get through to the daughter who resented him.

My mother came to Colorado on vacation. She left Hawaii after she discovered that her boyfriend had several other girlfriends on the mainland. This loss dredged up all the other losses, and she started to pick her skin until she bled. Alone in paradise, she dug into the pores around her neck and shoulders. They scabbed, and then she picked the scabs. She had scars streaking her back. A literal clawing. She sold her apartment and quit her job selling Mercedes-Benzes, the career she built after she divorced my stepdad. She flew to California for a road trip with her former sister-in-law, my aunt Denise. They were supposed to spend a carefree few weeks crossing the country in a convertible. Their *Thelma and Louise* trip, they called it, even after being reminded how the story ends.

But when my mom landed in California, the bad news about Frank was all over the phone and all over the family. Her time in Colorado became an emergency pit stop, one she was happy to make, but she couldn't stay forever, she said. She couldn't get too caught up. She needed to heal, and her income was fixed.

At Lindsay's, my mom showed me her back. She took off her shirt and turned around. Wide and white scars, whiter than her white skin, crowned her shoulders. Some were fresh and angry red. I ran my hands over her shoulders and back and felt the way they broke her up, and I said, "Oh, Mama. No. You gotta stop."

She put her shirt back on and said, "Don't tell anyone, okay?" My mother kept her heart and her pain to herself too. And somehow she ended up with a real mouth runner for a daughter. I am the one who let the cat out of the bag. I am the snitch who gets stiches.

On Christmas Eve, Frank was nowhere to be found. Phil told Lindsay that it was time to leave. Possessing his own expertise on junkies and thieves, Phil knew what was going on. He told his daughter that Frank was stealing his pain pills. He'd been counting, and every night there were fewer by a few. It was a pilfering.

He said, "That's what addicts do, Lindsay. They steal from you, and then they smile at you on the fucking stairs." He was angry. And as anger is often also fear, he was afraid for his kid. My mother understood Lindsay's desire to keep the family together and her children safe, but her pills were missing too. And Frank hadn't paid back any of the tens of thousands of dollars she let him borrow from her retirement.

Phil had been here before. His brother, our uncle Dennis, died a junkie, stealing and sneaking and smiling up and down Hancock Street, with the same dead look in his eyes.

Never mind jail, Phil told Lindsay. Leave now or you or the kids are going to find him dead.

My sister had lived her whole life avoiding this outcome. An addict for a husband. She believed the stories our parents whispered to us with fierce hope and belief: it is going to be better for you. And yet here we were, same country, different house. Which was not to say there wasn't growth or that our parents had failed us. They loved us, rough and plenty, and they showed us the trick doors and dark closets of the world we came from. It's just that they couldn't do anything to stop it from spinning exactly as it would.

Of course Lindsay didn't leave. She stuck around even as she grew to hate Frank. She loved her family, and he loved his kids. She got thinner in pocket and pants. She got gaunt. And no matter how much money my parents poured into the mortgage, the bills, the groceries—the money disappeared. The need was unending. There was a junkie inside the gates, rifling through the castle.

* * *

UNCLE DENNIS WAS NOT AS handsome or as muscular as his two older brothers, and he looked as if he was up to something. When he walked into a room, his eyes roved the faces, the women, the things he could steal. In his late twenties, he was already bald in the pattern of his brother and his father: the horseshoe of hair, the perfect, shiny head. He wore a mustache, as was the style. He was funny and quiet—the quietest of the Treska brothers by far. His face looked exactly like Phil's and he was short, like Bobby. Phil thought he might've been seriously unwell, like Loretta. Dennis would've been more attractive if he hadn't been an addict.

His heroin use turned into a heroin addiction, and then his addiction grew, as addictions do. It wasn't long before hocking stolen goods didn't cut it anymore. He needed big cash to feed his habit. He wanted and he wanted, and he wanted escalation.

Dennis also had something to prove. He saw the action that flooded Papa's diner. That action kept his brothers in enough cash to feed their hobbies and habits, and he wanted to assume his place in the Treska family business. But he was too much younger than them, and he couldn't get a word in edgewise. There wasn't anywhere he could go that his brothers hadn't been. He couldn't seem to make himself fit. He tried harder and harder, and his attempts became more desperate. His crew became unsavory; his habits, bad habits. Dennis wanted to be who everyone expected him to be—a Treska. But it was somewhere he couldn't get. It was a full boat by the time he turned up.

His fall was short and swift.

Dennis and his buddy robbed a Cumberland Farms in Belmont. From robbery to shoot-out took twenty minutes. It should've been a quick smash-and-grab for cash and cred, and it was almost that easy. The holdup went to plan, but they sped past a cop after the robbery report went through on the radio. They should have been more careful—back roads and speed limits and all that—but by this point, Dennis was a renegade.

The police officer hit his sirens, and my uncle pulled over—at first. Then he threw the car into drive and took off, Cadillac fast. He wouldn't slow down until he crashed. That was the thing about my uncle: no brakes and aimed for disaster. By that point, there wasn't anything anyone could do about it. This literal disaster only morphed his ongoing existential disaster into a reality. *Of course*, everyone said when they found out what happened. *Of course he did.*

The police were on alert in Waltham, Watertown, and Belmont as my uncle sped through each town, going eighty in a twenty-five. He flew down narrow neighborhood streets with kids and old ladies thick on the sidewalks. Dennis looped back and forth, hung Louie's, ran reds.

He turned down a narrow street in Watertown and found a barricade of police cars waiting for him. He could either stop or not stop. And so he slowed down—at first.

My uncle was behind the wheel, and he's the one who hit the gas into a line of police and cruisers. He's the one who drove them into a hail of bullets, one of which passed through the shoulder and out the back of his buddy. Dennis burst through the barricade and drove halfway down the block before he accordioned into a parked car. Dennis lived, and his friend who rode with him was dead.

The story ran on the front page of the local papers and on page 3 of the *Globe*.

Dennis never saw any of them. He went straight to the hospital, then straight to jail. If he had, he may have pored over the picture of the Cadillac, its long hood crumpled to the windshield. The windshield pocked with five bullet holes. He may have wondered how he survived.

Dennis didn't die. He lived and was sentenced to ten years for the robbery. He served five. My grandmother hid the rings and necklaces he stole in an empty ice cream container in the freezer. She was afraid they'd be seized as evidence, but no one came for them. Years after he died, Hancock Street was filled with the strange and elaborate trinkets Dennis had sold to his mother for drug money.

I have one of these rings—gold with a fat emerald in the center, surrounded by smaller diamonds. It shines and it is ugly, and I wear it. I will always keep it. That emerald ring holds our Treska glories and failures in its gold band. This Treska totem is the only piece of us I have, the only piece of my uncle. His hands were all over it.

When my grandma Treska pressed the ring into my hand, cold from the freezer, I was seven, and my uncle had been dead a few years. I felt the bevel pinch my palm. She held her hand firm over mine and said, "Take this, Nicole, but don't tell anyone. This was from your uncle, and he loved you so much. But you've got to keep it a secret, do you understand?"

And isn't it just the thing that I understood? Isn't it the power of secrets and shine that, drawn to both, I was willing to keep one for the other? And I did. I kept that secret for a long time. Conscripted young, that's the way they get you. A Treska is a Treska is a Treska.

By that point, my family had constructed Dennis the Myth. Dennis of Good Intentions. Beyond that, there's no speaking ill of the dead. In our family, there's no speaking of them at all. It hurt too much.

"I COULDN'T MAKE HIM DO what he needed to do," Phil told me, reclining in Lindsay's leather sectional, fighting sleep. Fighting everything. He never forgave himself for Dennis. For Loretta.

My uncle was twenty-four when he got his friend killed. He lived the next eight years, five of them in jail, a kid with a body count that he didn't come back from. It didn't kill him quickly, but I think it did kill him. What I do know is that heroin killed him, on the books. The rest was speculation.

"Dennis is a real sore spot in my heart. I couldn't get him away from people I knew would take his life."

Phil and Bobby were the last two alive. They talked more than they ever had before, which still wasn't that much. They felt almost like real brothers, for once. Veterans of a different kind of war.

My dad relived Dennis's life and death often, replaying his decisions and exchanges with his brother, his parents, the police. He dreamed of Dennis. The only time he loved a cop was when they told him Dennis had a gun, and could Phil come and get him before something bad happened?

Of course he would. Phil would've done anything to save him. But this Dennis he tried to talk sense into? He didn't want saving. This Dennis was already a hot ghost.

Phil hid the worst of his family from Lindsay and me our whole lives, not out of shame but out of heartbreak. The loss of a sibling was too big for language. Phil tried to make Dennis better; he tried to make him okay. But Phil was too late—a lot. He didn't want to talk about it. What was there to say? Look it up, he told me. It was all over the newspapers.

I emailed the Boston Public Library archives, and they sent me the articles that related to my uncle and the car chase. I pored over the details. The loaded Magnum, the Cadillac folded in on itself, the windshield and the bullet holes. All the facts laid out in black and white.

Twenty-four and twenty-two years old. To me, they were still babies. Twenty minutes from the moment they walked into Cumberland Farms to when the police put a bullet through his friend's chest. Twenty minutes to run the Cadillac at eighty miles per hour through three townships and back again. Twenty minutes to end two lives, one immediately, one eight years later.

My dad worried what I'd write about Dennis. It wasn't that he didn't want me to write about his brother, or what he'd done, or that it wasn't true. But it was hard. Dennis wasn't how he died or what he did.

My uncle overdosed for the last time in that apartment off Winter Hill. Every time we passed it, my father crossed himself and mumbled a prayer. My family blamed the guy he cooked up with for giving him a dirty hit.

Phil called it the Treska syndrome.

"What does that mean?" I asked.

He told me that it meant the horrors of growing up a Treska: "It's almost like a curse that Papa put on us," he said in the dim glow of Lindsay and Frank's mounted jumbo-screen TV.

It was his father's fault: he and Bobby agreed on that. And it wasn't the backhands or the beatings. Those they could deal with. What wasn't okay was how he put them in front of gangsters. Put gangsters on pedestals. Put that macho craziness into his children.

"It's a syndrome," my father said, "and we all have it."

Men and women can break and keep breaking, but eventually it gets hard to mend, to get back up. Some people give up, and some go crazy. And some people hit the gas, because they've run out of road and there isn't anywhere else to go.

To say it was my uncle's fault seems too neat. "Fate" may be a more graceful way to say it, and I'll ease toward grace because I can. I can look at my family and see much more grace was needed than this world provided. And I can grant Uncle Dennis grace because my parents did hard things to grant it to us. They bricked over their hurts to smile for us kids and teach us to ride our two-wheelers. They kept their secrets to themselves to let Lindsay and me grow free from the poison that lived in the soil of the places we come from.

ONCE, BUT ONLY ONCE, I took Lindsay to a support group for family members on heroin. We went in the week between Christmas and New Year's, when life is about as low and bloated and miserable as it plans to get. I figured this was the best time to convince her before I went home to New York. I had sent her links for months—websites for rehab, websites for support groups and hotlines. But she brushed me off when I asked. No, she hadn't gone yet. No, she hadn't called. She was busy, but she appreciated it. Thank you, she told me. Now, I stood in front of her with her coat in my hand and it was harder to tell me no.

Lindsay. I couldn't believe the tension coming off her. She was my baby sister, and I didn't know how to convince her that it was okay and not okay to be an addict. And it was okay and not okay to be married to one and not have known. It didn't mean she was like Mom, or that Frank was like Dad, or Dennis. Lindsay couldn't take a step back and see the big picture, small as she was inside a frame she didn't choose. She looked at me, trapped. Like, *What do you want me to do?*

The Nar-Anon meeting was in a conference room on the ground floor of a silver-windowed building off the interstate. Everyone there was the parent of a child who started on pain pills before moving on to heroin. Everyone in the room loved an addict. Lindsay was the only spouse. The group was small but close; they held Christmas parties and monthly dinners. A few of their children were dead. A few were in jail, and a few they'd let back in the house. They shouldn't have; they knew they shouldn't have. But this was their daughter, their son they were talking about. This would be the last time.

The group passed the tissue box around the circle. Each parent gave an update while the rest nodded with downcast eyes, supportive shoulder squeezes, and back pats. When Lindsay held the box, everyone turned our way. We were new; it was an introduction. I saw my sister listening to the others, who had also been overcome by the giant wave, the tsunami of American opioid addiction. I hoped she heard forgiveness, relief, and community in the circle, but I don't know that she did. I saw the tissue box shaking in her hands, and I'm afraid she saw defeat. I saw the wave suck all the water out of her shallows and tower over her best defenses.

"Hi, my name is Lindsay. My husband is on heroin. I have two kids, and I . . . I need help."

When a big wave breaks, the force is incredible. In that circle, Lindsay broke wide open. The rushing waters took over, and everything she held on to washed ashore.

My little sister was scared to speak of her fear, because to speak it made it real. Her pain was a whale song understood by those who knew the frequency. It was a choir that grew and grew, and everyone in that room wore the robes of the initiated.

Afterward, Lindsay went slack, slumped in her chair. Her tension was gone. I saw her exhaustion. She didn't want to stick around after the meeting. On our way to the car, one of the mothers pulled me aside and gave me her phone number.

"Please give this to your sister. I can see she needs to let it out. I hope she comes back. I think it's great she came."

I took this woman's hands in mine; we weren't strangers anymore.

Lindsay never returned to the group. She never called the support mother. Maybe her shame outweighed the camaraderie or the support felt like an indictment. She shouldn't be coming undone. This wasn't supposed to happen.

**YOU'VE GOT TO SUFFER
TO BE BEAUTIFUL**

*At Lindsay's cheerleading practice with the Red Devils,
Pensacola, Florida, 1990*

I **saw the Turk** for the last time over Valentine's Day weekend. He returned to New York at the beginning of February, and while we had talked, we hadn't seen each other in over a month. I texted him: "I miss you. I don't want to be a bother, and I don't want to be a fool, either. I just want to put that out there."

I was trying to be bigger than my fear. I was trying not to run or be silent. I wanted to say what I would regret not saying when it was over, the words I didn't know how to articulate. Me, the word girl. I wanted to be brave. More important, I wanted to sound *cool*. I was not pulling it off. The text read middle-management millennial—a thin veneer of girl boss to cover up the fear.

"Nicole," he said, "I understand your feeling, and you're not a bother to me, but I feel I can be one to you in my current mood."

I was afraid of being rejected but also of seeming crazy. The Turk and I talked for hours on end, and he told me how much he loved spending time with me. Then he disappeared. And then he came back. A time traveler, returned. And I always wanted him back. I didn't ask questions.

He was like every man I'd ever loved, fiercely lovable and expressly unavailable—this city girl's catnip, making googly eyes unavoidable. Historically, I saw that my father and grand-fathers gave so little of themselves yet cultivated real fan bases. I saw their bullshit and swore I would love a better class of man. But I didn't, and that made me feel crazy.

I met the Turk outside the Union Square pavilion that last weekend we spent together. The lights from the subway station lit up the falling snow so you could see it swirl in the dark. It was that romantic kind of winter night in the city where the wind wasn't blowing and it wasn't too cold.

I saw his feet before I felt him bump me, shoulder to shoulder, his hands in his pockets too. I looked up, and he leaned down and kissed me, his beard snow-flecked.

When he had texted that we should meet, I was face down in my bed, sure it was over. I was stupid in love with him, but I wasn't stupid. He delivered a poet's "it's not you, it's me," but that's what he'd said. I decided to try to move on. I reactivated my Tinder account to make myself feel better, but it did not make me feel better. Whenever I opened the app, I cried, hor-rified I would find his profile active again.

"Oh, hello," he said, easy like that.

We walked down Fourteenth Street. The snow formed little drifts and dunes over the garbage bags underneath.

Pointing to a drift of snow, he said, "It's enough to cover a body."

"I never thought of it that way," I said. Now I always think of it that way.

He stopped and watched snow fall on my hair, glasses, and nose.

"Should we go home?"

"Take me home."

We got on a train to Sunnyside and walked the ten minutes to his apartment holding hands and not speaking. We passed the Sunnyside mural that covered the long side of a brick building. It looked like an old amusement park sign, its cartoonish letters jumping off the wall, optimistic behind the blowing snow. Out his windows, I watched the storm roll over the square and out again, like dreams coming and going.

In the morning, I woke to find him still awake, shirtless, smoking, and playing *Genshin Impact*, an open-world video game that never ended. I stood behind him, my hands already tangled in his thick hair, streaked white.

He had spent the night traversing the edge of the video game's map until he found a platform where he waited for a transport balloon that never came. He said he wanted to enter the ether beyond the game's border. He met someone else on the platform, some other astronaut at the edge of the world. They chatted for hours about life and philosophy. He explained such an affinity for this stranger, this soul whose soul he certainly now knew. I found myself jealous.

Each day of our long weekend, I woke to go home. Each day, he asked me to stay. I held my boots in my hands and sat on the couch to pull them on, and he asked me to put them down. So I did.

•

WHEN I WAS TEN, MY mom took Lindsay and me to spend the summer at Henball's in Andover, an upscale suburb outside Boston. We went because Henball wasn't doing real hot.

She was up all night and in bed all day while her baby sat in pissy diapers and a pile of empty bottles. So my mom did what she always did with the people she loved who were broken: she showed up. She opened the windows and pulled back the white shutters, blew out the candles burning too low on the coffee table and turned on the lights. She dumped the ashtrays, found the Windex, and got to work.

I loved Henball, but I was nervous. I'd never seen her like this, and she could be mean to me. Henball was tall and lean, with thick sandy hair that she wore in shaggy bangs. She had a leather bomber and wore heels with jeans and always looked as if she had just pulled up on a bike. (Though she didn't have a motorcycle, most of the men she dated did.) Her expectation of everyone was the same as the gymnasts she trained: unquestioning loyalty and zero body fat.

I possessed neither of these. I questioned everything. And at ten, I was already tall and thick-thighed, with fat, young breasts that required a bra. I was a pretty child, but puberty turned me awkward with hormones.

A Harvey Edwards photograph hung in Henball's living room, behind a white leather couch. A ballerina in tattered slippers stood in fifth position. Duct tape held her slippers together; her burgundy leggings had holes, and her mustard tights sagged. The image was a celebration of endurance, of toughness toward beauty. It was a trait both my aunt and my mother admired. It was almost as if they couldn't conceive of beauty without great cost. Or maybe they understood everything came at a great cost.

In the kitchen, there was a companion shot, this one of a ballerina en pointe, her sweats hiked. One foot was bare, bruised, with her wrapped and broken toes exposed. The other foot wore an ivory slipper, satiny and perfect with ribbons. I spent a lot of time in front of those images that summer, wondering what they meant about beauty, and women. What they meant about me. I was already bigger than Mary Lou Retton, the gymnast who swept the 1984 Olympics and became America's darling. So what was I supposed to do about that?

It wasn't that I didn't believe in beauty; I did. But I didn't find suffering noble. I didn't want to break my own feet. When my mother brushed or braided my hair, she said, "You've got to suffer to be beautiful," and thwapped me with the broad side of the brush to stay still. I hated that.

Henball had an in-ground pool behind a white picket fence. I spent most of my days that summer doing cartwheels off the diving board, into the deep end. My hands kissed the pebbled surface. I bent my elbows, then locked them to ensure a good bounce. Some boys from down the street came over a lot, and we played in the pool and watched *Pee-wee's Big Adventure* in the living room while our parents drank in the sun. Pee-wee was a grown-up kid, or a childlike adult. He laughed and grimaced as he learned the funny, sad things about life and love, and I understood him. That summer, I watched the movie over and over on VHS, transfixed.

One day, the older boy, maybe twelve, asked if I wanted to go downstairs to the cellar with him and his brother.

"I want to show you something."

I said yes.

The stairs curved and creaked and the cellar was musty and damp, like all New England cellars. We descended into the dark and let our eyes adjust. The washer and dryer were next to each other, and a television sat on top of a table for folding laundry. A water heater clicked in the corner near the window that let in dusty light. The window faced the pool, and through the gauze of cobwebs, we saw feet moving back and forth. We were quiet. The older boy moved a chair next to the washer and dryer and held his hand out to me. I took it, and he helped me up onto the machines and lay me long over them. He pulled another chair over for his little brother.

The older boy lifted my top, where my training bra covered the humps of my swollen nipples. With great intent, he rubbed my baby breasts. He showed his brother where they bloomed red. Then he pushed his fingers in between my legs, the way I did when I was alone or with my girlfriends in the dark during slumber parties. I felt hot and hot and hot. He felt me pulse and heard me moan. His brother touched my nipples and rubbed them back and forth.

I turned eleven that summer, and I was filled with the new sexual ache of being eleven. I kissed my friends in our backyard tents, and we rubbed between each other's legs and came out red-faced and twisted up, guilty and thrilled.

Henball spent the summer teaching me lessons about men, but she hadn't taught me this. She told me that boys wanted to touch you under your bathing suit, under your culottes, under your parents' nose. And I learned from my mother, very young, that boys' want was a crime. She told me what had happened to her. She said, "Don't you ever let them touch you."

No one told me it was like this. Nice.

But I knew it would be.

My auntie told me that men liked it when you smiled. They

liked it when you gave them what they wanted. She said, "Remember that you're getting something you want too." I smiled up at the boys hovering above me. Their hands operated carefully, opening a current that charged the cellar, charged my life.

A chorus of "Eh, ohhhhs!" rang out from the pool, signaling someone's arrival, and we jumped, breaking the current that turned me slick. We went back upstairs to the movie, and I lost myself in the feeling of being touched.

The night before we left Henball's for the beginning of a new school year, we ate dinner around the big oval table. The baby covered himself in spaghetti. We laughed big, and my mom poured me a few sips of red wine. In the world we came from, that whole gentle summer—swimming and laughing, the bright kitchen with the black-and-white floor, the air moving sweet through the open windows—all of it was tender and full of love. We were together, healing, happy. After dinner, my mother put the baby to bed, and Henball and I cleaned the kitchen. She did the dishes; I stacked the plates and swept the floors.

"Nikkabella Chickanella, come here, let me show you a trick women need to know."

I looked at her. *Had she spoken with the boys' mom?*

I moved toward the sink to learn more of the ways of women.

"This is what you do when you're done with the dishes. You take the dish soap and run it around the sink like so."

She took the Palmolive and swirled electric green all over the porcelain sink. She grabbed the sponge and wet it, scrubbing down the sides.

"See? Elbow grease. Especially after eating meat. The fat sticks. Now show me, and rinse it off."

She handed me the sponge and watched me move it around

the steep sides of the sink. I used the retractable sprayer to rinse and my free hand to keep the water from spraying onto the counter. Another woman's trick.

"See, when your guy takes you over to his parents' place to introduce you and you have dinner, you go into the kitchen with his mother at the end of the meal and do the dishes. Then you clean the sink like this at the end of the night, and they'll know you're a keeper."

•

THE TURK AND I KEPT each other warm that last weekend. We watched YouTube videos of British and German labor songs and argued about which were better. When I offered up Kendrick Lamar or Beyoncé videos as a contemporary response, he told me I was cute and booped me on my nose. He said things like, "I know hip-hop is political," while closing my laptop and reaching across my body to fondle my breast.

I went home on Tuesday night. I took my lonely train ride certain he would reach out the next weekend. And then the next. And then the weekends piled up, quiet as snow dunes, until I felt certain he wasn't going to call at all.

When the Turk left me, I hid and hurt in private, like an animal. And when it was too big to bear, sometimes in public. With my tears and repetitions, I wore my friends thin. I made dates, had bad sex. Rinsed and repeated. I tried to time travel too. I thought maybe I could find my way to a life with love in it.

DANGEROUS ANIMALS

My mom and me in Estero, Florida, April 2016

n April, I visited my mom in Estero, Florida. It was spring break and I hadn't spoken to the Turk in two months. I arrived in Estero understanding it was over, and I wanted to hurry my hurt. It was preferable to holding it at bay and creating a sinkhole of my heart. But I couldn't hurry my heartache, so I went searching for comfort from my mom.

Estero sat on the Gulf side of Florida, north of a seven-thousand-acre swamp. The air choked you, and everything from the bugs on up threatened to eat you alive. Hurricanes routinely flattened entire towns along the Gulf. I had been in the state less time than it took a python to digest a full-sized human, maybe a little longer than it took to die of heat stroke, and already I felt the rising panic that Florida and family put in me.

I let the sun warm my winter-paled cheeks. *This is going to be good,* I thought, settling into the taxi's wood-beaded seat. *I deserve this.*

On the highway, twelve lanes of concrete refracted light, and souped-up street racers cut in and out of traffic, accidents waiting to happen. The cabbie yelled, "Quiet, Jockey!" to the cars as they darted past, their mufflers *bratbratbrat*ing. Feeling my heart thump in my neck, I listened close for skips.

"Okay, this was a mistake!" I yelled into the front seat. The driver took her eyes off the road and threw them at the rearview for a dangerous long time.

"Well, it's too late now, girl."

Cyprus trees lined my mom's subdivision; their roots fanned out for balance and broke up the sidewalks. Up close, I could see rust bubble through the carport's white steel roof. A golf course sat behind the blocks of white condos, and a water trap was visible around the back.

My mother waved from under the carport. She wore shorts, a T-shirt, house slippers, and a long sweater she held closed with her free hand.

"Christine-y Bean-y, I have arrived!" I shouted out the taxi window.

"It's no-see-um season, Nickabella! Hurry up and get inside. You know what they say: 'You can't see 'um, but you can feel 'um!'"

I did not know they said that.

The living room was empty but for a couch—long and velour with tasseled fringe and deep cushions. I dropped my bags and myself onto it, obliging an itch behind my knee.

"Don't you love this couch?"

"It looks like a soft place to lie down," I said.

"Oh, it's basically brand new. When old, rich people die, their furniture ends up in consignment shops. You know Mama always finds the best deals. Have a nap, and I'll get us dinner."

When I was growing up, my mom took us to Marden's Surplus and Salvage most weekends. In the car, we sang the jingle, our vowels long and high: *shoulda bought it, when I saw it, at Marden's.* We went to fire sales and estate sales and auctions in barns and church basements. She sewed our clothes and canned and jarred and jellied everything she could get her hands on. In a New England summer that is plenty. Lindsay and I grew up with a childhood happiness neither of my parents had known. That was the hand of my mother. Out of nothing, she made beautiful lives.

I fell into the twitchy top of sleep on the dead-people couch. My mom turned up the television in her room to retirement loud. Murder show sirens and the far-off pops of golf balls permeated my dreams. I stopped checking my phone for texts from the Turk, but I saw him behind my eyes.

When I awoke, I was alone and dusk smeared the sky. Tiny red pox had appeared on my legs like constellations, and when I ran a full-body inventory, I found a new, angry bump on my arm that twitched along with my pulse. Then I found more. By the time my mother returned with dinner, I had a list of suspects and was zeroing in amid endless theories online.

"A spider, maybe? A centipede? Are those even in Florida? They must be; they're awful. Everything awful is here."

Florida blue centipede. There it was. It was grim. The sheer number of legs and intentions, stunning. The no-see-um bites were one easily identifiable thing. This bump, really more of a lump, was another.

On the Internet, I found and memorized the lyrics to "Please Don't Let Me Die in Florida," a song I discovered searching for ways I could die in Florida. It wasn't a good song, but my interest in it was largely conceptual. My itch, though, was visceral: a need that almost touched my bones, a frantic scream that spread across my limbs. I had my own skin under my fingernails. *Please don't let me die in Florida.*

If I scratched deep enough, I could get to the bottom of the thing and rip it out. Have a good look before it shriveled under the butter sun. But I couldn't get there. It was more like a sneeze that never came, a tease that hurt.

"Did you know Burmese pythons are one of Florida's most invasive species? And there are classes to teach you how to kill pythons? Like before they kill you?" I said. "Did you know there are cash rewards for dead snakes?"

My mom never indulged what she called my "overreactions"; she thought I made a big deal out of everything and told me as much. She dismissed my current concerns with a tired "Oh, Nicole, come on" and made coffee. This was a Boston response to any suffering short of a gunshot wound or five fingers to the face. It was hard to hurt around people whose survival depended on looking at life and death with shruggy apathy. It was hard to have big feelings around people who suffered so big there wasn't much you could do to compete. And I was sensitive. And this rash was sensitive too. And spreading.

She changed the subject and told me how she'd stopped dyeing her hair the same bright red she'd had since she was a little girl. My mom was a tiny half-Irish kid with an Irish bum for a dad in an Italian neighborhood. Her Italian mother punished her for this all their lives. My mother carried my grammy's pain. Both of them were little girls who had endured too much. My grammy had five kids before she was twenty-five. One of them, Robert, died at three months old. My mom was the only girl with three brothers, but she survived. And they did not make it easy.

I saw my mom as a young woman, making the moves and the money she needed to escape the dark corners of tough neighborhoods like Maverick Square and Jeffries Point. I see her running drinks to Italian mobsters and running them to the hospitals, their guts in their hands. My mother, their little sweetheart, their personal Madonna.

I see her grown and running books for my dad, for the Winter Hill Gang. On the phone, shooting the shit, her voice was laden with the expectations she didn't need to verbalize. She took bets from East Boston to Southie. Her code name was Max. And while she might've been five-foot-nothing, it was very true to say she was, and remains, mean when she's mad.

I see her hearing what Bianca's husband did to Henball's boyfriend, and trying to control her face and her racing heart, thinking of her baby girl at home.

I spent my adolescence in the sprawl of the American suburbs, afforded by my mother's decision to get us the fuck out of Boston. We moved between bases and coasts and split-levels and cul-de-sacs for fifteen years with my stepfather's career in the navy. My mother grew up in projects, and she chose our homes based on their school districts. Health care and education were the greatest luxury, and she lavished them on us. I went to high school with people whose parents were teachers, and engineers at Lockheed Martin, or worked in sales or HR in vague, isolated office centers. Those shiny office cubicles always looked lonely to me, but the world was bigger than East Boston. They meant minivans, two-story houses with walk-out basements, college test prep, and other affordances I had no fluency in.

A family around a kitchen table reading the newspaper and asking for someone to pass the salt was a parody in my house, meant to be aped and eye-rolled. Oh, fucking *please*. We were the salt, and we were screaming. In the suburbs, my friends' parents were slow and graying by the time their kids hit middle school. They wore clothes from big-box marts. They bought their decor from those same stores and their food too, which ran off the labor of their neighborhood's criminally underpaid. I don't remember what any of them looked like. Only the sameness and the smiles.

MY STEPDAD, DADDY MIKE, FIT right in to this new life. He took us to fairs and carnivals in the summer, where we went on all the kid rides and into the jumpy houses. Phil Treska did not go in jumpy houses. Daddy Mike had been a gymnast at the University of Maine and wooed us city rat kids with his back handsprings that culminated in twisting flips, his arms tight to his body, his body high off the ground.

Mike was from the deep woods of Bethel, Maine. He was from a place with horses. He met my mom when his stepbrother dated her half sister. His brother went on to become the town pimp in Bethel, with "Mr. Lovely" tattooed on his ass cheek. Daddy Mike's people were *country*. My mother often pointed to their framed picture in our living room and said, "We're not related to them."

In my best memories, Daddy Mike still had a full head of curly hair and wore a striped polo shirt. He had a mustache and cool sneakers, and we bounced to "We Built This City" by Starship in the blue light and shivering peaks of the bouncy castle. He loved being stationed in Brunswick. "The city," he called it. The pace and tastes of the suburbs suited him.

But not us: we were kinetic. Wilds into the wild. My stepfather could not tame what he married: a part-time bookie and her two Albanian kids. We roamed the American suburbs, the lot of us a terror. My mom had an asymmetric haircut and wore leather bomber jackets when she picked us up from school. She was the coolest woman in the strip mall, loud and cursing around the straights. My mother reveled in her loud laugh in the restaurant and PTA meeting—her casual "fuck you" at whichever discount department store in whichever state.

Could families that didn't form against a fist or fight to find their place even be families? What bonded them? What held them up, these families that didn't scream and swear in love and rage?

For all her domestic inclinations and aspirations, my mother was forever a city rat. She told her stories with a far-away look and a mother's reserve. They were unbelievable and exciting and heavily censored.

"See?" she cooed, from our poor corner of the suburbs, down the road from the wealth and influence of a very different class of people. The suburbs, where things weren't great, but better than they might be. "We're important too."

I knew why my mom moved to Florida. It was a dangerous place, and she'd known more danger than I could imagine.

"Nicole, get a grip; you just got here. You need to smoke a bone and get to the beach."

Turning back to my search results, I mumbled, "Oh, I'll get a grip, all right. On your neck." In Florida, trees lived in brackish water and snakes from those trees turned up in toilet bowls.

If you are hurt by any of the animals on this list, seek medical attention immediately.

I looked at my mother over the laptop. The list was long.

There were black bears in Florida. That seemed excessive. My mother wasn't worried about the bites, but then she never was. She went out on the porch to smoke and watch the golfers finish the back nine.

I scrolled an image search—a horror of poxxed dermises in furious shades of pink—looking for a bite pattern that matched mine. As I did, an email notification pinged from the tenants' rights lawyers appointed to my case. They had reviewed my lease and found sufficient grounds to move forward with a suit against my landlords.

My LAWYERS RAN A NEIGHBORHOOD cooperative, and they kept incredibly busy filing suits against landlords for wrongful destabilizations, egregious claims of eminent domain, and rampant neglect. They'd seen a significant uptick over the last few years as landlords exacted their available pressure and wealth to speed Harlem's gentrification. These lawyers were in their twenties and thirties and tattooed and passionate and idealistic and free. As in, they didn't cost anything, which was imperative. Even though I'd finally found financial relief in my rental bedroom, I still couldn't afford a lawyer's hourly.

The law project had a high turnover rate, and my case had been reassigned to several different lawyers. A new associate told me I shouldn't pay any rent increase until they had gone over my apartment's rental history. It looked likely that the apartment had been illegally destabilized a decade before, the year the rent doubled with no capital improvements reported. It was the oldest trick in the book, the lawyer said. But it was still a gamble to pursue a lawsuit, and I had to be aware of the potential for loss.

If I lost, I would be beholden to the arrears on the slip, which would increase by $400 a month, as well as the legal fees of all seven owners. I would also be out of a home. But the way I figured it, I was being priced out of my home anyway. At least in this scenario, I could fight. I could stay in my apartment until I figured out what to do, a luxury of time I didn't always have. The lawyers told me to expect the arrears to go up and up and up. And although this was a tactic to apply pressure, I could find myself on the hook.

I was born on the hook. What was I, if not a gambler's daughter? I knew how to writhe.

ON MY FOREARM, THE RED bites swirled hypnotically.

My mom's condo sat on the fifteenth green, the grass crunchy and dead, the water feature murky. Fat men in white shorts strolled past, glowing in the near dark.

"You know, Nicole, Estero is a *gated* community."

The gate, the green, and the white pleased my mother and made her feel safe. Not so for me. In fact, quite the opposite. Florida dissolved me in its warm waters, leaving only the hard pillars of my fears. Even inside the gates, *especially* inside the gates, there were bites. Inside the gates, there were panic attacks that rolled between breaths, like waves.

"Yeah, I saw that on my way in. More of a wooden arm than a gate."

On the porch, my mom didn't look up from her phone. She wore a big T-shirt and sat on a plastic chair with her legs crossed.

Up and down her calves, light blue veins spider-webbed away from and back into each other. She was beautiful. Her hair fell thick in front of her face. Since she wasn't dyeing it anymore, the crown of her head glowed white. She looked both youthful and aged at the same time. She looked like retirement.

I admired her calm the way a mongoose might admire a raptor—impressed but not to be trusted. In love with, but terrified of. Florida was full of dangerous animals. *Some people are more comfortable here than others*, I thought. And scrolling her tablet in her underwear, my mom looked awfully cozy. I raked her fingertips over the lump on my forearm. "Maybe," I said, "we should go to the doctor."

If you catch me dying in Orlando . . . The night frogs outside had a way of singing that made me hate their singing. *Throw my bed onto a traiiiiiin . . .* The screen vibrated between us, clogged with tiny no-see-ums caught and panicking. The myth was that my mom broke the cycle of abuse, when in reality she still hurt us.

"You know what, never mind. You're probably right. I need to smoke a bone. I'm sure it's nothing. Occam's razor and all that," I said.

My mom looked up for a moment.

"Occam's razor? Never heard of it."

I couldn't be sure, but I suspected the smile that turned my mom's mouth was mean. Cruelty was a survival tactic where we came from. There was power in it. No one ever validated my mother's hurts, so how could she know how to validate ours?

Once, many years later, a therapy session drifted to my mom's casual cruelty.

"I don't understand," I told Lisa, my therapist, "why I keep letting her hurt me."

She said, "There is the myth of the relationship you have with your family, and then there is the reality. They are not the same. And it's the distance that causes dissonance."

But I knew she loved us. Once, she told me, "When you were a toddler, the horrors of my childhood came back and I wanted to drown myself in the Charles and take you with me."

She wanted the river to envelop us both because she didn't trust anyone else. I thought about my mom and what she thought about me; I wondered if she saw us at the bottom of the river, our hair floating toward the surface, no need for air.

I closed my eyes: longer than a blink but shorter than death. This was so hard—mothers and daughters.

"You don't know Occam's razor? Maybe you can give it a google. Maybe start looking up funeral homes while you're at it."

"Oh, Nicole. Don't be ridiculous," my mom said.

She was right. I *was* being ridiculous. That night, I fell asleep on the coffin-long couch, a contrite child desperate to negotiate. With each drag of nails across broken skin, I promised *someone* to do *something* if only they would make the hurt stop. I checked my phone before I went to bed. A blue glow leaked out from under my mom's bedroom door, and the screams of murder shows lulled us both to sleep.

I woke up in the dark, and the TV was off. The hard little lump had turned into a golf ball, and a rash spread halfway from my forearm to my armpit. I was certain it was an infection headed for my heart.

I touched the bite and thought of the unavoidables in my life that buzzed and stung. I rubbed the bites with the pads of my fingers to minimize irritation. Scratching caused cellulitis, which led to blood poisoning, I read. More blood poisoning.

And blood poisoning on top of blood poisoning was too much for any one body to handle. I looked up urgent care facilities, more plentiful in Florida than Publix, and ran the various routes until the sun came up, awash in information.

The next morning, at the urgent care located 0.08 miles from my mom's house, the doctor ran his index finger along the bundle of tiny red pimples that swirled like the start of a universe.

"This isn't an infection," the doctor said. "It looks topical. Does it hurt?"

"It hurts all the time."

The doctor made that doctor noise of terrifying interest—a forceful suck of breath exhaled in a "hmmm"—and pulled my arm under the light.

I heard my mom in the waiting room, talking to the woman next to her about how hard it was to find a medical office in Florida where anyone spoke English. The woman wore the orange-hued, spiky gelled hair typical of the area. She played a fruit game on her tablet with the volume maxed out. Bells sounded at surprising intervals. My mom maxed out her volume too, up and over the fruit game, to embrace the whole waiting room. She spoke to them about her inability to communicate.

"This is America! Where we proudly live and speak English!"

I emerged from the exam room waving my prescription like a flag.

"Bedbugs!" I shouted, victorious.

"I'm sorry, is this an exterminator's office or a doctor's office? Let's go," my mom said, pushing me out the door. In the parking lot, I could see the no-see-ums swirling in clouds when the light hit right. The air was miasma—teeming with scent and living stuff. It made a nervous girl more nervous to step out into it.

On the drive to the pharmacy, artificial beauty, safety, youth were advertised on billboards and in the malls: strip, open air, or standard. Estero's facade was blooming and new in direct opposition to the age of its inhabitants.

"It used to be only worker bees lived here, but in the last twenty years, it's built up into something nice."

It was a phrase she hadn't used before. *Worker bee.* She said it with the zeal of the converted. It seemed this population moved down here because they didn't do subtlety.

I didn't respond and looked out the window, where the car lots and chain restaurants recurred. This averted gaze was mine since childhood. It signaled distaste and dissociation. If there had been a door to shut, I would've shut it. The silent treatment was my equivalent of leaving the room when I couldn't. Or wouldn't.

"Oh, Jesus, Nicole. There's nothing wrong with 'worker bee,' it's cute. You don't always have to be so sensitive."

I spent my time waiting for prescriptions looking up complex reactions, salves, histamines, and associated fatalities. I read this information to my mother in the pharmacy drive-through and again while eating sandwiches on the patio at Panera.

About half the people bitten by bedbugs have no reaction whatsoever. Maybe a puncture hole, or a red dot, and usually that's it. Other people can get impetigo from scratching the itchy wheals that emanate from the bites. In rare cases, panic-induced heart attacks have occurred. The Internet said one guy died.

I displayed my arms, exhibits 1 and 2 in bas-relief. It's absurd, this need for fight. But without it we'd go mad and fall all the way apart.

"Am I sensitive? It would seem so. But maybe now's not the best time to bring it up."

ONE EASTER BEFORE PHIL WENT to prison, my mom got into a fistfight with his second wife when we were visiting Boston. This lady had a big house outside the city in Peabody. She threw parties in the backyard with Tab soda and badminton and yard darts. We'd never seen yard darts before. *Our* neighborhood adults played bocce and dominoes. I remember the darts in my hand, with a dangerous weight. Lindsay and I didn't know what to do with that kind of space, and we ran through it wild. She said as much and compared us to that city rat of a mother of ours.

We were staying at my grandma's on Marginal Street when Phil and his wife came to pick up Lindsay and me. The new mrs. must've said something sideways or grabbed our dresses too rough, because my mom sent her off the stoop with a clean shove. On the sidewalk, my mom leaped, swinging and screaming. Never more eloquent than in a rage, the things my mother said.

My mother.

Phil's women.

Even when they were high class, they reeked of the neighborhoods we came from. That's why they typically disliked Lindsay and me, with our thick accents and our mullets. It was always like that in Boston. The first or the only ones to get out didn't look back or they flashed off in front of you. It's hard to be poor and come from a poor place, to want more, and then get it. Sometimes it made you a real asshole, and sometimes assholes got their asses kicked.

By the time Grammy Duca made her way down the steep stairs and out the front door, my father had lifted my mother off the ground, pinning her arms to her chest. A familiar move. He held her back while his new wife climbed into the front seat of the car. Lindsay and I were already in the back seat. None of us saw Grammy coming until she came through the window. It was terrifying to behold. Phil's wife really got smacked around. She got a real East Boston beating, just like one of us. She wasn't so special. We weren't so different.

"You think you can come to *my* block, in front of *my* house, and hit *my* daughter?" my grammy shouted.

Each *my* punctuated with a slap.

When Grammy stopped swinging, her salon-coiffed hair was uncoiffed, a sight we had never seen, not even out of the shower, not even in a pool, not even in the swirlie chairs at Great-Auntie Christine's hair salon on Bennington Street. She opened the back door and pulled us out of the car. My dad drove away, his new wife screaming. We three generations of neighborhood girls caught our breath on the stoop. Our perfect curls fallen out.

AFTER ONE OF OUR FIRST moves as a military family, a kid hit me on the playground. I told my mom I was afraid to go back to school. She met with the teacher and the principal, but the bullying continued. So one day, when I got home, she set up pillows on the couch and stood next to me. She showed me a fighter's stance, arms up. I was seven. I think we lived in Virginia.

She held her fist closed, with her thumb outside—*always keep your thumb outside, Nicole, so you don't break it on someone's face*—and showed me how to throw a punch. She twisted her fist. The turn gave it oomph, made it more aerodynamic.

My mom said the next time I saw the kid, walk right up to him and punch him. Unprovoked. Retaliatory. Strike first to strike last. We practiced throwing punches until bedtime.

The next day I got on the bus and saw the bully sitting with his friends. He was two years older than me, but we were young, and two years still towered. I took my fighter's stance and shouted, "Hey!" and twisted my little fist into his face. He left me alone after that. What better skills could a mother give a daughter?

Years later, in high school, I was at my friend Tamara's house in Colorado. It was my seventeenth birthday and we were taking bong hits in the basement and watching the 1996 Atlanta Olympics. Kerri Strug had won gold on vault by sticking her landing with a busted ankle on live TV. We cheered, and after her coach, Bela Karolyi, carried her off the floor with such tenderness, we cried. We were full of wonder and weed, pride and patchouli. Just kids.

The phone rang, and it was for me. My mom said, "If you don't get back here right now, I might kill her." Lindsay, she meant. Lindsay was fourteen and had lied to her about riding in cars with boys. When my mom found out, she attacked her.

My friends didn't get phone calls like that. I knew my mother wouldn't kill my sister. But I also knew there had been violence, and there might be more. I walked the twenty minutes home, through the giant deadgrass park, open and full of thin Colorado air that was never enough for me. I considered Kerri Strug. Suddenly it felt wrong that she'd had to hurt herself like that. For what? For whom? I followed the main road that wound through the housing development until I arrived at our cluster of Lanes and Courts and Ways.

It was over by the time I ran up the stairs and into Lindsay's room. My mom was holding my little sister and saying she was sorry she'd lost control. The rest of the night we snuggled and practiced love and tenderness. It was new to us. We did Lindsay's homework together and cracked jokes—jokes that sort of pointed back to what had happened and let us laugh about it until it felt okay.

BACK AT MY MOM'S CONDO, I found more bites on my legs and bloodstains rusted in the seams of the new couch. It was my blood. I swore I was running a fever, but my mom refused to feel my forehead. I roared in the living room, my fists balled, and I shoved the couch toward the patio door. My new bites swelled into little mounds, and the puncture points raised up into sick little nipples. I showed them to my mother. It exhausted me, parading my wounds like that. I started to push the couch onto the patio.

"You probably got bedbugs in that filthy city and brought them to my clean house!" my mom yelled as I threw my weight into it.

How was this my fault? I thought, scratching my thigh where it itched. I felt new bites bloom in a tightly bundled bouquet. I counted them with my fingertips, but I couldn't tell one hurt from the other. I tried to read them like braille, but all they transcribed was: bites, bites, and more bites.

There was no denying things were as wrong as I thought—I'd been ghosted, and I had giant hives emergent. My heart broke; my skin broke. I bled. I picked at what had scabbed over the night before and cried. I cried about the bites, but also about the Turk and how little I, and our time together, meant to him. He disappeared the same way he arrived. Out of nowhere, in and out of time, like the man from *La Jetee.* But that wasn't true. He was still there, just not with me.

I felt some aperture of understanding being wedged open, like my mind had been dilated, and I saw the truth, too bright. Starbursts and coronas. Explosions of understanding went off in the dark chirping Florida night, a tilt-a-whirl gone off its rocker. The Turk didn't want me anymore, and he didn't want to tell me, and so he wasn't going to. It meant that little to him. *I* meant that little to him. I was crying. I was crazy. How could my mom not empathize? Her heart, her skin, had been broken too. I'd seen her scars.

I scratched my arm and blood dripped onto my hand. I pinched and scratched and sliced each bite with my nails without realizing I was hurting myself. *I must be allergic to bedbugs,* I thought, miserable.

For some people, bites take weeks to manifest, fueling the anxiety that attends a bedbug infestation. You never know when you were bitten. It's hard to know if the bugs are still there or if they're gone. I knew the red inflamed hurts on my thigh would go through kaleidoscopic changes before they eventually disappeared, but other worries crowded my mind.

What if the bites follow me back to the city and into my bed?

What if I mistake the cornsilk flowers on my soft sheets for that which crawls?

I went back in the living room and took my clothes off.

Crazy women run in the family, I thought, naked and bleeding and crying. Auntie Loretta lost her mind, and I wondered how close to the ugly edge I wandered. My mom seemed unconcerned, having put up with enough of my shit.

"What if I lose my mind?" I asked from the floor.

Red flags were planted up and down my arms and legs. I tapped an invented code of surrender on my thigh.

"Nicole, honey, I'd say it's a bit late for that. Put some clothes on. The exterminator just pulled up."

It was the first good news I'd heard in days. I rushed to pull a dress out of the dryer, full of hope and Benadryl.

Ken the Exterminator's haircut was a high-and-tight, like a Marine, and he was blond. My mom approved of all of that. He wore blue paper booties over his shoes, and I approved of that. *Booties, right. Smart.* Finally, someone was taking this seriously. Bedbugs were hitchhikers, the Internet said, and I could see Ken didn't want to take them home with him, either.

He took a special flashlight and examined the baseboards and rugs. He looked at the mattresses and the box springs, pulled up the seams, and peered into cracks. He examined the couch on the patio and pointed out quarter-sized rust stains.

"I can't see anything here. Bedbugs are lazy. They don't travel if they have a host, and it looks like they found one in you."

He holstered the flashlight a bit prematurely for my tastes.

New Yorkers were on vigilant lookout for roaches, bedbugs, mites, and smaller mites, and I would've preferred a little more rigor.

"Well, since I can't treat what I can't see, I'd say getting rid of the couch is probably good enough," he said.

"You can treat anything, Ken. If you really want to," I said. "I've spent a good deal of time and money treating what I can't see."

I held my fingers in the crook right under my jawbone, self-monitoring for arrhythmia, palpitations, revving. I checked for these things since before I knew the words for them.

I said, "You know, there's a shrimp right here in Florida, the mantis shrimp, that lives in the shallows and sees sixteen cones of color. Humans only see four. These tiny, tiny shrimps. They see so much more than we do. We're limited, Ken. That's all I'm saying. More limited than shrimp."

I talked fast, gesticulating. I was sure to be the youngest person dying in Estero. I looked to Ken for comfort, my eyes full of galloping horses, but he stood there blasé in his booties. In fact, the whole of Florida didn't seem to give two cheap fucks that I was going to die staring up at the Spanish moss with no-see-ums in my open eyes.

"That is enough, Nicole," my mother said, her fearful smile fixed on Ken.

I found a cold justice emerging down in the swamplands; there were alligators of indifference at every turn. Maybe my mother was right; maybe I did this to myself by fucking too many foreigners.

"Ken, you're not single, are you?" my mother asked.

Ken nodded in the negatory with an unearned familiarity.

"No, ma'am, I'm married with a little one. And I'll tell you this, I feel confident enough to let my boy sleep here. My own child."

With that, he handed my mom a pink invoice for the consultation, the payment information circled in red marker. He brushed off his shorts, top to bottom, and stepped carefully through the screen, leaving his booties inside the door.

"Married with a little one, Nicole. You hear that?" My mom scratched absently at her leg, under her shorts. That morning, I told her the Turk and I spent hours that turned into days and months together, and then nothing. Nothing at all.

Her voice stood in the empty room longer than it might've otherwise, and her words spread over the tile like something spilled.

Bites. Before they faded into stains, they formed heads that burst and dripped amber syrup—impossible not to pick and pick until they bled, until they scarred. I starfished myself on the living room floor again and yelled at the ceiling, at my mother.

"Listen to me: I wouldn't marry that idiot if his cargo shorts were stuffed with a million dollars. I wouldn't marry Ken if he was the pied piper of bedbugs. Which, by the way, he is not. He couldn't catch a bedbug in a house made of bedbugs."

From the floor, I swirled my arms around the place to indicate we were in such a house.

Bites. Whenever I visited my mom, this was what happened. *Why do I do this to myself?* I thought. Every time, I found myself floored, on the floor. Bitten and bleeding.

LOADED

Friends in Amagansett, New York, August 2016

That June, I went to Spain to visit my best friend, Catherine, for two weeks. We met in the summer of 2010, when we both attended famed editor Gordon Lish's writing workshops at the Center for Fiction in the Diamond District. Over the years, our friendship grew as we scraped by in love and publishing. She had moved to Bilbao in the spring with her curator boyfriend, Manuel, who accepted a job offer at the Guggenheim Bilbao. Manuel was a handsome Spaniard who wrote decent criticism. He took Catherine to Spain with him when he got the job at the museum, but he already had his eyes on bigger prizes. Catherine and I were both a bit blinded by these men we thought were brilliant. So blinded it took us too long to realize how little they cared for us.

After I left Spain, Catherine found emails confirming her suspicions that he was sleeping with gallery girls all over the world. But even when I arrived they felt tired of each other, working opposite schedules and only overlapping for dinners, which were tense. Manuel and I never got along. He didn't think I was beautiful or important, and I thought he was a self-absorbed asshole long before the cheating came to light. I found his definition of beauty too shallow for him to be any kind of authority. We stayed out of each other's way. Catherine and I spent those weeks on our own, eating small plates of tortilla and stuffed squid, bacalao croquettes, Iberico ham and Romanesco. *Pintxos.* We drank spritzes around little tables and smoked in squares until four in the morning. Bearded Basque men in tight pants smoked, sang Basque songs, and paid no attention to us.

So, unplanned as good things often are, the summer after getting dumped and eaten alive in the swamp was a glitzy affair. It was a summer that took care to show me the expansiveness of the world that felt hidden in the small, single-resident town of Heartbreak (populous a place though it may be).

I needed a big, expansive world. After eight months of hosting tourists, I was cooped up. I had dishpan hands. Tourists and their same-same song and dance had worn me out.

And I was growing uncomfortable with Airbnb's rapidly expanding business model. The company claimed to help people and build strong communities, which was true enough at first. In the beginning, Airbnb ran more like a glamorous couch-surfing website than what it quickly became—a corporate vacuum that sucked housing off the market.

By 2016, fewer and fewer listings on the website advertised shared rooms. Most were for entire apartments being rented out as hotels. This was happening worldwide and creating a shortage of available housing in most major cities. Berlin outlawed short-term vacation rentals and imposed five-thousand-euro fines for residents who broke the rules. Other cities considered following suit. Though New York was not one of them, I was being priced and pushed out of my own apartment and I didn't want to contribute to anyone else's problems. So,

I switched gears. I took down my Airbnb listing and booked my bedroom exclusively through Columbia University's housing portal, a website that matched students in need of lodging with renters. I rented the furnished room, all in, for $1,500. Mostly international PhD candidates and postdocs messaged me, in the city for a semester to study.

Booking guests for longer than a month meant less maid duty, but also less money. I wasn't making a hundred bucks a night anymore, but it was enough to cover most of the $2,100 in rent my lawyers advised I pay my landlords. The rest of the rent and the bills came to around $1,000 a month and I had money left over for leisure and savings and rest. What luxury. I bought economy-plus plane tickets to Spain and Hawaii. Ahead of my thirty-seventh birthday, I opened my first savings account with the Airbnb windfall, seven thousand dollars. I bought a custom-made linen dress and left for Europe with a beautiful Italian postdoc studying linguistics staying in my apartment. That summer, she and I both had it made.

TOWARD THE END OF MY two weeks in Bilbao, I went on a Tinder date with a Spaniard. I wore my new dress. He may have also been a piece of shit, like Manuel, or maybe he was a saint, like in his profile. I'll never know, but I let him eat me out in Catherine's vestibule and take me back to his place. In the morning, he made me coffee. He played *Sketches of Spain* by Miles Davis and sucked my nipples as the Nervión River flowed past his open windows. He fucked me one more time, then put me on a trolley on his way to work with no intention of ever calling me again.

I slipped into the apartment and found Manuel on the wooden bench, tying his shoes. They were old, but he polished the scuff out of them and took care to line them up by the door; I noted the way he hung his leather jacket and folded his clothes. He valued his valued possessions. I also noted the way he yelled at my best friend about frying the peppers wrong, making the coffee wrong, and buying the chicken wrong. I noted how she was a skinny girl gotten skinnier.

He knew I'd spent the night out and why.

"Do you want to live in a foreign country with your foreign lover, like Catherine?"

"I would take parts," I said, casting a meandering eye over his receding hairline, "but I'd leave others." We tight-smiled past each other and I went to bed, the long French doors open to the same river I'd rolled with earlier.

I left Spain satisfied. And it wasn't only the sex. It was how I moved that summer. I came and I went. I passed through. I felt good. I was my most comfortable self: wandering and watching, wondering how to be, trying to be that for a while, then moving on. I fell into the habits of my childhood and found comfort in the pick up and go. I enjoyed the friends and the fucks and the spinning wheel of the world. I remembered that my life was expansive. That hearts broke, but they also bounded.

In July, I went to Oahu's North Shore for the wedding of my friends Jael and Cessi. Jael and I went to college in Honolulu together, and thirty of our friends came home, or came north for the wedding. We stayed in cabins on the water and ate and drank and did nothing together for a long weekend. Hung over, or about to be, we let the ocean lift and release us in her swells. We smoked blunts and tiptoed naked across the bioluminescent reef. We knew it wasn't right, but the underwater lights were so brilliant. We drank taro bubble tea and ate Dole whip pineapple ice cream and loco-mocos, a local favorite of fried rice topped with a hamburger patty and a fried egg, smothered in mushroom gravy. I hiked Maunawili Falls Trail and went to La'ie Point with the friends I grew into adulthood with.

When I was in Hawaii, I was someone different. Maybe more myself than any other version of me—the me I'd become in the early aughts, baby-adult Nicole. I rode BMX bikes and smoked cigarettes in low-rise miniskirts. I pedaled up and down Kamehameha Highway without *slippahs* and listened to Eve's "Let Me Blow Ya Mind" on my iPhone speaker.

This freedom I'd hustled to afford healed me too. I felt an ebbing of the pressures and constrictions of New York and my heartbreak. In Hawaii, my toes spread from only wearing *slippahs*, and I felt the way I often felt in a place where I'd lived but wasn't from: home and not home. Inside and outside. I felt that, too, in Boston, the home I was born to, and in New York City, the home I'd chosen.

That summer of movement and joy and inside-outness was part of this new life I discovered that I didn't want to give up. Enough money meant ease and comfort and affording a good life that felt good. I understood that in the abstract, but I had never known having *enough*. And the more I saw, the more I wanted and wanted.

* * *

I MOVED TO HAWAII IN 1999, right after my twentieth birthday. Daddy Mike got stationed at Kaneohe Marine Corps Base on Oahu, and we lived all over the island—Hawaii Kai, Kailua, Kaimuki, and Kaneohe. I ran the counter at Boston's North End Pizza Bakery, owned by (East Boston expat? exile?) Big Tom Rossi. I went to Kapiʻolani Community College before transferring to the University of Hawaii in 2000. In Honolulu, I encountered real wealth, generational wealth, for the first time. It was hard not to. Big money and inheritances abounded: mansions, private schools, luxury cars, country clubs, and celebrities. It was blinding.

I worked at the Outrigger Canoe Club on the east end of Waikiki. This was after I had graduated from college, the first member of my family to do so. The club's members included descendants of the families that had stolen and colonized the islands, and their children ran blonde and rich through the slatted tables in their Sunday best. Old white women stood in lines and stiffly hula'd as the staff, largely local and Native Hawaiian, stood behind the serving stations and watched. Many of my friends went to Punahou, a private college preparatory school where Barack Obama went. Some were members at the Outrigger. I had to serve them.

While I waitressed, those same friends were off to graduate school on the mainland or working office jobs and building their careers. I could feel the slip happening again. I was falling behind in the very same moment I had surpassed the academic accomplishments of my family. It was that Boston shit all over again: too good for this side of the river, too city for the other.

Phil visited us in Hawaii twice a year and stayed for three

weeks at a time. He stayed at what he called the Polynesian Palace, a rundown pink motel surrounded by high-rises off the beach in Waikiki. The interior was vintage rattan furniture upholstered in worn aloha print. It was Christmas all year long at the Polynesian Palace, with dusty fake Christmas trees and ever-twinkling lights. Aunties worked the reception desk, and the rooms were situated around a pool that was dingy but private. The room my dad got sat above a Korean BBQ, and the smell of sweet potatoes and mandu dumplings floated in through the windows. It was a Treska kind of place, which meant I had to explain it to my friends—my friends who would go on to be lawyers, and pilots, and professors.

One visit, driving into Waikiki, I asked Phil why he went to jail.

"I was dealing drugs. You know that."

"I know I know that. But what did you *do*, exactly?" It felt unbelievably bold. The code was no one told anyone anything, ever. But that only made me want to know more. My dad, maybe too drunk, maybe too old to care anymore, said, "I was working for the Winter Hill Gang, you know, with Whitey Bulger."

We sat at a stop sign, about to turn onto Kalanianaole, the highway that turned into the H-1 Interstate and ran Oahu east to west.

"Whitey Bulger? You worked with him?"

This, I thought. This was news I could use. I could turn this into something new. I felt the myth shift, reorganize, ascend. I couldn't wait to tell people my father was no ordinary criminal but a credentialed one. Everyone knew Whitey Bulger; his reputation was indisputable. Terrible, but indisputable. Whitey, the Ivy League of mobsters, and, here, my dad, an alum.

I rearranged the cards and saw a better hand. And, hey, a gambler's daughter is a gambler's daughter.

"So you were like Boston royalty?"

"Oh, yeah, you could say that." My dad was also being re-invented as an object of interest to his daughter—a man with interesting stories to tell. "I mean, your mother waited on those guys pregnant with your sister. Howie Winter himself congratulated me when I got out of prison. I did time for him, Nicole. And I never flipped on anyone. I did good time."

We headed east into Honolulu, our sunburned arms out the window of whichever beater car I drove at the time; they were all junka-lunkas. The windows didn't roll down, or the windshield wipers were stuck at twelve o'clock. Maybe bungee cords held the bumper on, or duct tape held the hood down. One junka lunka caught fire on the Pali highway, and another dropped its engine block on Mariner's Ridge. A third junka lunka required the battery be disconnected to turn it on or off.

We drove past mansions and Jaguars. The median of banyan trees formed a canopy with those on the sidewalks, and the trade winds blew cool. I peppered my dad with questions as we turned down Kalakaua Avenue on our way to the hotel. My father interrupted me.

"Listen, Kid. Let me ask you this, and don't say nothing to your mother or your sister. You think you can loan the old man two hundred bucks? The Palace froze my account until they run the final charge. I didn't know they were gonna hit my card like that. I have to get through the next few days, and my check comes in on the fifteenth. I'll give it back to you when you come to Boston. I promise."

We idled in front of the motel, the engine humming into a hiccup as we sat there, quiet.

"Yeah, of course I can. But I need that money back. I only have two thousand dollars, and I told you I'm going to be in Italy for six weeks. I need the money."

"You think I would take money from my daughter without paying her back? What kind of a father do you think I am?"

In my baby book, my mother wrote in neat cursive, just like my grammy's, *Honey, your father took your christening money. Mommy wrote this in pencil, so that when he returns it, I can erase it.*

AFTER MY SUMMER OF LOVE, I was back home in New York, and my friend Eugene said we needed one last, shiny weekend before the anxieties of fall arrived. August was for last chances, he kept saying. So we drove to his family's house in the Hamptons, a place I'd never been before.

I had met Eugene years before when he dated my friend, the one with the dating spreadsheet. (This was a fact of great and terrible interest to Eugene upon discovery.) While the spreadsheet failed to deliver them a romantic connection, it did have its strange magic, and after they split he and I became great friends.

His family left the Soviet Union in 1990 and settled in New Haven, then Seattle before moving to New York City, where his father was an immunologist at a major hospital. We bonded over being displaced kids very aware of the currency of coolness—its ability to mete out credit, to open doors. We were scrappy little urchins who learned to get by.

When we pulled up to his family's big, modern home in

Amagansett, white and angular, I said, too loud (always too loud), "You live *here*?"

I WENT TO GRADUATE SCHOOL at City College with a forty-year-old who wore faded Neutral Milk Hotel T-shirts and faded hoodies. Once, he invited me on a lunch date with his family. I was surprised when he told me to meet him at the University Club in Manhattan, a private club founded in 1861 by some dudes from Yale.

In my years in New York, I learned it wasn't always possible to tell who had money just by looking at them. That was a per-petual surprise to me. Why would anyone want to be seen as poor? Or dress poor? I spent my life escaping it.

Like Gatsby, I wanted to reinvent myself in New York, as someone better, from somewhere better. Like Ripley, I wanted to evolve until you couldn't see my poor anymore; my design choices, impeccable. My summers in Europe involving a yacht. But I also knew life didn't work that way.

At the University Club, they peppered me with questions about my family, and I offered up answers. I leaned over the King Arthur table to deliver our myths, our punch lines of pain. His stepfather was ancient and in a wheelchair; his mother was much younger and still a beauty. The wood of the tables was three inches thick and polished to such a high gloss I could see my face reflecting back at me, uncomfortable.

I left lunch feeling like I'd given them what they wanted. I'd fed them, but I was still hungry. I realized I could break down every door that stood between me and the libraries and balconies, the fluency of criticism and culture, and it wouldn't matter. I could learn the names of the chairs and cheeses and the painters and how to say "It's all a little too much" in French, and everyone would still know which side of the river I came from.

I SPENT THAT LAST SUMMER weekend in the Hamptons watching French reporters and Yale socialists shuck oysters and discuss the children of the Bush administration. We did drugs at the beach and laid around the bonfire barely dressed and running our hands over each other, high on "Floor Molly." One of the scientists had acquired the drugs from another scientist, who ensured its purity and strength by promising we'd spend the night on the floor. We talked about it for weeks with delight. None of that speedy shit. This would be perfect.

And it was.

I played *Pet Sounds* by the Beach Boys and *Loaded* by the Velvet Underground. The bonfire threw its bright oranges and yellows over our bodies and the water, and the whole bay spun to the twinkling, lovelorn melodies. Like a carousel.

It was beautiful. And everyone was beautiful (both on and off drugs), wearing robes of silk or cotton or nothing at all.

In the morning, we ate scrambled eggs with butter and tarragon on sleek red couches. An Englishwoman who had been a reporter in France and now worked for the UN said she hadn't spoken to her parents in years. I sat up and yelled across the clean, empty living room, "Wait, really?!" so loud it boomed into the upstairs bedrooms. I was always so exactly myself, especially when I was trying to be someone else.

"Yes, I spent years going round and round with them. I figure I suffer with or without them, and less without them."

Rhetorically, I understood anything was possible. But in reality, I couldn't see it. Or, rather, I couldn't see a reality where I wasn't walking around my apartment with my phone on speaker loud-talking one sibling or parent through one crisis or another. And yet here was this beautiful, sophisticated British woman without a bra telling me something else entirely.

I wanted to come from a lithe people with carefully crafted thighs that could crack walnuts. I wanted the clarity of mind to be able to reason my way through and away from my family. I wanted plate collections and inlaid bookshelves, inlaid wooden floor, an inlaid life. I wanted to be free.

I leaned over to Eugene. "I don't trust any of these people." He smiled.

"It's okay, Nicole. They don't trust you, either."

HA-HA ON THE BEACH

Phil and the toupee, Father-Daughter dance, Brunswick, Maine, 1989

One Thursday in October, Auntie Ha-Ha called and asked me to come visit her in Winthrop. Maybe the rhythm of the summer's movement hadn't left me yet, or maybe it was because Ha-Ha was my favorite person in the family (which made sense because she wasn't actually a member of our family), but I obliged. That semester, I was teaching Advanced Grammar, a class that met at 5 p.m., and after my last class of the week I hopped on an Amtrak bound for South Station. More than a year had passed since I went to Gloucester with my dad, and I wanted to hear the boats and lobster traps tap-tapping against wooden docks. I wanted to go home.

Ha-Ha had been a runway model for Jordache, and her billboards were all over East Boston and downtown in the eighties. She talked with a transatlantic accent and dated my mother's older brother, Uncle Joe, for a few years, then stuck around. That's how they did it, these East Boston anchor girl-friends who became my mother's friends and my aunties. She used smooth rocks from the beach to crush garlic cloves, and dressed as Marilyn Monroe every Halloween. She swirled into cars and restaurants wearing furs and long gloves and smelled like flowers I couldn't name. Her laugh tinkled *ha ha ha* like some sort of aristocrat.

Although she was only ever a five-minute drive from Grammy's in East Boston, Ha-Ha felt worlds away. Her house smelled of butter and weed, and she woke me up with joints and tangerines. She called me Nikki Nou-Nou and told me I was beautiful. I loved her like crazy. She helped me see that language and laughter could be soft, a revelation in the hard place we came from. Auntie Ha-Ha wasn't compromised the same way we were. She was elegant and existed right in the middle of our bullshit. She was a marvel to me.

Ha-Ha always lived out by the water in Winthrop in some big airy apartment, on streets with whimsical names like Mermaid Lane or Seashell Way. Winthrop was just east of East Boston, across the Saratoga Street bridge and out toward the water. The homes were big with wide porches, and those on the coast sat on stilts or piling to protect them from winter's surging waters. The kids in Winthrop went to parochial school. When I arrived, in a cab from South Station like some sort of adult, my auntie handed me a joint and told me they were moving soon.

"To another apartment? Or *moving* moving, like out of the city?"

"Yes, my love. Out of the city. Where it's quiet and we can have a house. We can't afford anything here anymore." In East Boston, there were high-rises where there used to be train tracks along the water.

My auntie had married a nice Irish guy a few years before. After he served his time for bank robbery, he joined the pipefitters union. With his thick accent and stories of glory, he was genuine and kind and took care of my auntie.

Ha-Ha and Uncle Bone were my only family left in Boston. Bone bounced around single-room-occupancy rooming houses and drank himself skeletal. He wouldn't answer my phone calls.

I had first, second, and third cousins, aunties, and uncles scattered around Boston and the rest of Massachusetts, but we hadn't grown up together, and I didn't know them like that.

It was only Ha-Ha left.

WE WERE ON HER BROAD back porch that smelled of low tide and citronella and a bit of mildew. Boston was unseasonably warm. She held a crystal glass in one hand, a cigarette in the other. Ha-Ha told me the Doggie story again.

She liked to tell me how my stuffed doggie got the hole in his stomach, the ragged tear my mother covered with patches of old bathroom towels.

"Your father trotted you around Somerville and dealt drugs out of your little stuffed doggie. You know that," she said. Auntie Loretta had given Doggie to me, and I carried him everywhere.

Every time, my face turned incredulous. I didn't know if I believed the Doggie story anymore.

Ha-Ha said, "Well, how do you think that hole got there?"

"I am of the mind that I loved a hole straight through to his stuffing," I said.

She laughed in that way my family laughs when I reveal some naivete born of a lie my parents sold me cheap.

"What? Mom told me. I snuggled him raw!" I said.

Truth be told, I could see my father pushing me around the neighborhood and stopping in front of one of the houses on Hancock Street to yell from the sidewalk, that trusty city doorbell, and wait for someone's son or uncle or brother to come out the chain-link fence and onto the shared space of the street. Some guy he'd known his whole life. They'd shoot the shit: who was in jail or pregnant or dead. Everyone young but old already. Veterans. Everyone in tracksuits, or Lynn tuxedos as they're colloquially called—named for nearby "Lynn, Lynn, City of Sin," as it's also colloquially called. You know the type: sometimes windbreaker, sometimes velour, but always zip-up, always vertical stripes.

I told Ha-Ha what Phil said when I asked him about the Doggie situation in Revere the previous summer. He shot me a grin, a dazzling flash of admission and pride. It was pure vanity, pure Phil, and then it was gone. He said, "Listen. I need you to believe me when I tell you: I don't know anything about that. But if it did happen, it wasn't my fault. I would never do something like that to you, to Doggie. He was sacred to you, so he was sacred to me. And if I did it, your mother told me to do it. If I did it. Which, you know what, now that I think about it, I don't think I did."

My mom was incensed when I asked her. She said, "Nicole, what kind of a mother do you think I am? Do you think I would let your father use you as an accessory? Get the fuck out of here. You slept with Doggie every night. You rubbed your little face in his belly. You think I would let your father put drugs anywhere near something you loved? What kind of mother?" she asked again.

"Believe what you need to believe, my Nikki Nou-Nou," Ha-Ha said. She pointed out that my family loved to lie. She said people from places like ours didn't always do the right thing, and then told themselves and everyone else all kinds of reasons why it wasn't that bad. This was done to protect us, the kids, she said. And she wasn't wrong.

My mom said, "If we stayed in Boston, I don't know if my best efforts could've saved you. Nobody who stayed there came out all right. But you kids did. I made sure my kids did." And she wasn't wrong, either.

She snuck Doggie out of my bed once a month to wash him. I took him to the playground and ate my meals with him. I drooled on him and lay sick with him. My mom mended him when my love and the washing machine wore him thin and tatty.

I know she wouldn't let my father use Doggie to sell drugs. And I'm almost positive my dad wasn't ever stupid or high enough to do something like that. Aren't I? But then there was Phil, smiling and backpedaling. And here's Ha-Ha and her story. Why would she make something like that up?

My mother said, "Who told you this? Ha-Ha? Oh, right. How many drinks did she have when she told you? Who are you going to believe, me or her?"

And that right there was part of the paradox, part of the problem. My whole life I was asked to believe someone and suspect someone else. I was always being told so-and-so didn't know what they were talking about. Or they were lying.

Who was I gonna believe, that guy?

What was I, stupid or something?

Often both were true.

My auntie was smoking and flicking her ring finger against her thumb, looking at me like, "Come on, Nou-Nou, don't be an idiot." The truth seemed clear, but that old familiar feeling of doubt was clearer. I wondered how much the truth even mattered anymore and lit another cigarette.

I said, "You know, I took a bus to Maine a few years ago. I went to one of those islands off Portland's coast. Close to our old house in Brunswick. I didn't even know there were islands out there. Anyway, we came up Route 1, and I had this urge to turn around and yell, *This is where I grew up* to the whole bus. I didn't realize I felt that way. I barely come home anymore."

My aunt smiled and said, "I think the evidence of your being a Bostonian, darling, might be your insistence on announcing it to an entire bus. What do you think?" And we shook the porch with our ha-ha's, legendary henballs in action.

MY MOTHER, HENBALL, DEBBIE, HA-HA—THESE women formed my life, with their pillbox hats and fishnet stockings, their shoulder pads and hairspray. There was nothing godly or neat about them. They were the women whose authority and confidence would drive my own. They cut the air and seduced it and left every room bleeding and charmed. And, Lord, were they loud, each a holy organ with magnificent range.

There is a photo somewhere of my mother and her girl-friends, arms wrapped around one another in a pose that is both familial and decidedly defensive, a phalanx of sisters. I was in the middle of this explosion of tuille and chiffon and silver teeth and chunky rings, with my little leg out, my little dress hiked up in one hand. There I was, tucked into their skirts, dying, always dying, to belong.

Phil's best friends too. Those Somerville gamblers and scammers who wore tracksuits and gold chains and neck braces and loved me and my sister and slipped us fivers and taught us to swear. Billy, David, Richie, Tommy. City guys, all mouth and two-finger points for emphasis. They're dead now, but they taught me too.

Accept what you've been given: that was our credo growing up. I imagine it was how most people who came from secrets grew up. I don't mean people *with* secrets; at least those people knew something. That was their power. I'm talking about the people who were kept in the dark to be kept safe. People like me. I think People with Secrets tend to make People of Secrets, thinking that it's in our best interest, and it probably is. But the problem is you can't stay in the dark forever. And then what do you do with all that light?

HA-HA OPENED ANOTHER BOTTLE OF wine and asked, "And how is old Guido Sarducci doing, anyway?"

Guido Sarducci was a *Saturday Night Live* character from the late seventies. He was full of shit and shit excuses—a real "check is in the mail" type of guy. Phil Treska was also a real "check is in the mail" type of guy. In Boston, nicknames were conceptual and referential, delivered with great emphasis. Your nickname revealed a preciseness about the bestower and the bestowed. As a kid I used to call Phil Guido Sarducci, too, understanding it meant a swaggering, full of shit, ambiguously southern European. A very good nickname indeed.

"He's not great," I said. "He'll be out in New York next month for his birthday."

"He was never great," my auntie said. Ha-ha.

"No, I mean, he's in between homes. Not even homes— short-term hotel rentals in Florida. It seems like he's running out of money since he went to help Lindsay."

"Yeah, well. That's not your sister's fault. He's been running out of money his whole life."

BRUNSWICK WAS AN IDYLLIC PLACE to be little. It was a place where Lindsay and I built igloos out of the snow that piled high to the roof gutters in the winter. We used big wooden shovel-buckets to rake up blueberries by the pound in the summer. We skied and rode horses and did other unusual things for city rats, like climb trees and have stairs *inside* the house. Rhubarb grew wild and abundant out our back door.

We were only a two-hour drive from Boston, and our family was always over, spilling out of the driveway and into our cul-de-sac. Daddy Mike was a new officer, young, handsome, and a real rules guy. (My mom swung sharp in the other direction after she was free from Phil and Boston and the mob.) He did everything by the book and thought that if he studied enough, he could get what he wanted. He was usually right.

My family teased him relentlessly. They pulled up to his garage in jean shorts on motorcycles. "Look at this guy," they teased my mom, too, with their feathered hair and their spike heels and their chain-smoking and doing-coke-in-the-half-bath kind of ways.

"Look at this hick," they said, pointing at him with their cigarettes. "Who the fuck does he think he is, anyway?" They drank his summer kegs of beer. They slept on his couch.

The first thing Phil did when he got out of prison was come to visit us in Maine. I ran to him, excited he was back from camp after so long. He greeted me on one knee and waited for Lindsay to follow, his arms out big. She hid behind my mother's legs and shook her head no no no. She wouldn't come.

"Lindsay, it's me," he said. "Come on, it's your *fatha*, don't you remember?" he said, mostly joking but also a little scared.

Of course she remembered him. Of course.

"Come on," I said, calling to her. "That's our dad."

I remember thinking she was being naughty. But she was only a toddler when he went away, not this gangly kid who loved Joan Jett and She-Ra and had a will to match. My mom said Lindsay was born with an animal sense of other people and her surroundings. If she didn't feel safe, she ran. She wasn't so different from the rest of us. Lindsay screamed, "No!" and disappeared into the dark house, leaving my father on his knees.

A FEW YEARS LATER, PHIL drove up to bring us to Boston for the weekend. He arrived wearing a new toupee. Chestnut with blond highlights. The toupee covered up his horseshoe baldness, the signature glowing head. We gawked. But even we knew better than to say anything. It was too much vanity, too much shame to address directly—Phil and the rug.

So we stood in the driveway and greeted him as if nothing was wrong. He walked from his Cadillac, which was parked against the sidewalk, our address spray-painted on the sloped curb. He did the Phil Treska thing of pulling at his collar and waggling his neck when he was nervous. He was strutting, but in a way that revealed deep insecurity.

Perhaps this is the only way one strutted.

But that day, it was amplified. His nervousness sang in the zip of his shiny suit pants. It blew in the breeze that caught his new, full head of hair, or something like hair.

"Phil, look at *you*," my mother said, and it was devastating.

My father's gait took a hit, but he carried on, unbowed. He had nowhere else to go. My sister watched my mother look at my father, and she saw the way he dented. She ran to him.

"Hey, Kiddo!" he said, and stooped to sweep her up with great relief. It was unusual for her to show him affection, let alone the bounding kind. It couldn't have come at a better time, a more necessary time. He was dying in the driveway, getting cut down by friendly fire, by gazes meant to kill.

But not this time. This time, he would survive. His kid was running to save him and give him the grace to stay on two feet. He swooped her up, around, and into his arms. At almost seven, Lindsay was all legs and too lanky to hold for long. But before he put her down, she reached her hand as if to cup his face. Instead, she flipped up the front of the toupee, revealing the wig's white mesh and the glue on my father's bald head. His scalp tacky now, and not glowing.

"Surfin' in the USA!" she shouted, and turned to my mother and her girlfriends in ecstatic frenzy.

Henball and Ha-Ha knew Phil at his most charming and at his most abusive. They fed us when Phil canceled the credit cards. They served him the divorce papers. There was no comfort to be found in that yard, not for Phil. Only the high and sharp kinds of cackles that get you nicknamed Henball and Ha-Ha in the first place.

I shouted at the women, deep in their lawn chairs, their feet up on the beer keg, their toes perfectly cherry red: "Don't be mean. Stop it! That's mean what she's doing! You're encouraging her! People are going to hear you."

Their howls rang around Independence Drive. My father saw what his daughter thought of him. And for the first time, my sister saw it too.

One of my aunties (unimportant which, but probably Henball) said, "Oh, Nicole, who the fuck taught you encouraging?"

I suppose that was why Phil went broke paying Lindsay's mortgage and watching the kids. It was penance. To Phil, being there for Lindsay absolved him from what he did or didn't do when we were young. But of course, that's not how time or family or forgiveness work.

I hated the way our people hurt people. I hated the way it felt to be hurt by people who loved us but didn't know how to, so they said so with fists and stinging bites. That pain, that *Oh, Nicole*; that *Oh, Phil, look at you*. It devastated me from the time I was a little girl. I didn't want a nickname that cut me to the quick. I didn't want affectionate jabs. I wanted gentle places and soft words.

But from many years and miles later, I could see the shape of love under all that hurt and ridiculousness. I could trace our affection up and down those highways and backroads and drawbridges and rest stops and diners and end up home again. In Boston, I was home, even when there was no one left. I wasn't some lost child. Boston would always be mine, and I would always belong to Boston. Neither time nor distance could diminish that. It was my life too, splashed all over those street corners and the archives of the *Boston Globe*. That my name didn't exist in those pages was no diminishment (a fear I kept to myself). Instead, it was a testament to my mother—to her love that kept us off corners and out of the newspapers and jail.

I left Ha-Ha's on Sunday and took the train back to New York. The crispness had returned to the autumn morning air, and out the window, Massachusetts foliage blurred by in brilliance.

Phil would be in New York in two weeks, and I still didn't know when he arrived or from which airport. I called him to find out what he wanted to do for his birthday. I told him I was heading home and that Ha-Ha and I got drunk and high and laughed about the toupee incident.

"Jesus Christ, Nicole. Do me a favor. Don't tell anyone about the toupee, okay?" he said, without telling me his flight information. I told him I loved him and hung up without promising anything.

GUIDO SARDUCCI

Family portrait, Hancock Street, Somerville, 1981

Phil **arrived for** another birthday, on another Veterans Day, days after the 2016 election. I had been invited to an election-night-party-turned-photo-shoot at Russian Samovar, in Midtown. The party was hosted by Spencer Tunick, a photographer famous for his large-scale portraits of nude models posing en masse in notable places around the globe. He had previously photographed election parties for Obama versus McCain in 2008 and Bush versus Kerry in 2004. It seemed like a historic time to get naked and celebrate, so I said yes.

But the Turk had been right about the election, about America. I watched as state after state on the jumbo screen lit up red for Trump, and then I left the bar. There would be no naked celebrating. Not for me, anyway. I took a cab to Eugene's on Fourteenth Street. His election party was also on the rocks. We watched the outcomes together in silent shock. People left one by one, dazed. In my memory they walked at a slant, like ships rocked by a storm.

I wondered if the Turk was still in New York or if he'd gone back to Turkey. I didn't think of him every day anymore, but when I saw Erdogan on the news, strongmanning around, I worried about the Turk's safety. The next feeling was shame. Why did I care about him when he didn't care about me? I had been foolish and naive in our conversations about politics. I felt shame again. Was that why he left? I remembered the Turk's question to me, pedantic, exhausted, professorial: Do you know what kind of a country you live in?

How had I been wrong about so much?

I hired a car to pick Phil up at the airport. When he called to say he'd landed, I told him the keys were under the doormat, and that he could get into my building when someone else came in or out. It would be easy.

"You hungry, Pops? I can order you a pizza from the place right up the road or get you cold cuts delivered. What do you want?"

"No, Kiddo, don't worry about me, I don't need anything. I'm gonna lie down on the couch and we'll have dinner when you get home."

Phil was the kind of guy who said he didn't want to be a problem—didn't want to bother anyone—but at the same time, he did. He really did. He was a man of a million questions and needs. He didn't know how to work the air conditioner, the shower, the toaster oven, the French press. He got frustrated to the point of destroying property that he couldn't find Netflix on the remote.

I knew this, but I said okay and see you soon; I didn't ask questions. Sometimes I took a lie at face value. I allowed myself to believe my people were okay when I knew they weren't. I did that, I think, because they were never really doing okay, and I needed to live a life without drowning. Also, so many of them lied.

After my evening class at City College, I picked up a bottle of wine for myself and a bottle of brandy for my pops—E&J, the big bottle, as requested. I ordered the pizza. My phone rang before I went underground to catch the train.

One of my attorneys was calling to let me know that there was good news and bad news. The bad news was that my case was stalled while another tenant's case, *Altman v. New York,* moved through the state supreme court. The *Altman* case challenged landlords' ability to change the status of rent-stabilized apartments. Once destabilized, landlords could rent units at or above market value, which were approaching an average of $4,000 a month.

The outcome affected the active cases of about fifty thousand New Yorkers with claims against their landlords, mine included. If the case was decided in favor of tenants, it would mean thousands of people stayed in their homes. If the landlords won, even fewer rental protections would remain in place for New Yorkers.

I asked my lawyer what that meant for me. He said it meant everyone had to wait, tenants and landlords alike. These things took time. They wended and they waned, and court dates were mere suggestions. He told me that in his gut, Trump's election didn't bode well for tenants. Powerful people were taking powerful cues from his victory, and he expected things would get worse before they got better.

The good news was I could take the rest of the year off from worrying about my home; there wouldn't be any movement on the case until well into 2017.

I stood on the corner of 135th and Broadway, outside the train station, and considered the stack of rent receipts on my coffee table and the rising arrears. The most recent receipt said I owed over $2,000.

"I don't see that happening. But I take your point," I said.

I rode the train home and thought, *At least this buys me more time.* It was still a luxury to make my own decisions. I told myself and anyone who would listen that I wanted to leave on my terms. I'd been told when to leave my whole life. This time, I could say no and mean it.

I didn't have a new roommate coming until January and found myself with a guest room for my dad. But Phil was sleeping on the couch when I got home. His laptop bag and Patriots sweatshirt were on the bed in the second bedroom, next to his clean towel and washcloth, folded neat on the corner.

When I opened the door, he leaped up, half asleep, his glasses askew, one arm off his ear, the other pointed at the ceiling.

"I'm sorry! Hi. It's me, Nicole. Go back to sleep."

"Jesus, you scared me, Kid," my father said, the fear of war forever in him.

I dropped my tote and purse and took off my waterproof boots, the cashmere scarf I stole from Marshalls and my black Patagonia winter coat. It was down-quilted and had a zip-off rain jacket, and I'd worked a month of extra shifts at Pangea to earn the $500 to buy it. It kept me warm for endless winter blocks, and I thought it made me look smart.

After I lost the layers, I was lighter and more grounded— more myself. I looked at my dad. His pupils were pinpoints. He seemed relaxed and less needful than usual. I wrote it off to a day of travel. *He's groggy from the flight,* I thought, and opened the wine and brandy in my kitchen. I talked to him from around the corner.

"The pizza should be here any minute. You must be hungry; there's nothing to eat in this house." I decided I would tell him about the lawyer's call when I sat down.

"Hungry? I'm starving!" (Two words, with his thick accent: *stah-vin.*) "I ripped this place apart. Nothing! I looked on the counter, and in the cupboards, in the refrigerator, nothing. Thank God I found those brownies in the freezer."

I stuck my head into the living room, bottle of wine half-opened in my hand.

"Dad, what about the brownies? How many did you eat?"

The brownies had so much weed in them that I relegated them to the back of the freezer for the occasional, desperate chipping away. Even then, better to be careful. How high any particular bite might get you was anyone's guess. I treated those brownies with respectful wariness. I was too scared to eat them and too averse to wasting drugs to throw them away.

I joked that they were strong enough to take down an elephant.

Even stoned out of his mind, my dad was very aware of how people perceived him. The tone in which things were said, the length of glances exchanged; these nuances were policed and cataloged, then analyzed in his crazy mind. Phil saw my panic climbing and replied,

"What? One! I only ate one! I was *stah-vin*! What's wrong with them? I ate two, okay! I ate two. Why didn't you tell me?"

"I didn't expect you to go rifling through my freezer and eat the rock-hard brownies in the back! You told me you weren't hungry! Look at you, my god."

"Don't worry about me, Kiddo. Get me some pizza and a pillow and it's goodnight Phil. You think the old man hasn't been stoned before? You get my brandy?"

I saw the weed working in him, and I watched him fix his glassy eyes on this or that point in my apartment, He looked over at my bookshelf in lamplight.

"Look at you. You're the smartest girl alive, Nicole. My daughter the genius. Tell me this, Kid—do you think people can change?"

"Oh my god, Phil, you're so high. This is incredible."

•

AFTER I LOANED PHIL THAT two hundred bucks in Honolulu in 2005, I stopped in Boston to visit the family before heading to Italy. I was twenty-five with barely three thousand dollars and the wrong shoes. I'd never left the country before.

Phil swore he'd return my money, and I was eager to collect. I wanted to erase the pencil marks in my mind. Also, I needed the cash.

Henball picked me up from Logan, and we smoked a bone outside the old gymnastics studio in Orient Heights, where she used to teach and I used to tumble, across the street from Donna's and Ruggiero's and the Victory Pub. Our old, familiar haunts. Henball told me the bar's owner had a stroke after locking up one night and lay there for three days on the sticky floor. He survived and still wiped down the bar and the sticky bottles. He still emptied the ashtrays and wrote down your drinks with a golf pencil, just infinitely slow.

Phil was living in Somerville, again, on Central Street. He had an apartment in the basement of an enormous house that occupied a whole corner. It was that rust red of Massachusetts houses built in the late seventies and early eighties. At one point, it had been an enormous single-family home, two triple-deckers wide. A concrete path ran from the sidewalk through the chain-link to his door. I hadn't been to this house before.

Phil had moved into this basement apartment after divorcing his third wife, Lucille. They'd lost their apartment to gambling.

Lucy.

Phil and Lucy were together for seventeen years, his longest relationship. Lucy was sweet and so good to Lindsay and me. She loved to drink white wine and Sprite and had soft, cool hands and a soft, cool voice. She played the slot machines in the tribal casinos near Marlborough. Her eight great aunts lived together in East Boston, unmarried or widowed. They lived in the same triple-decker where they were born, before the Callahan Tunnel was built, and then above it. Their back porch was streaked with the lights and grime of endless cars coming in and out of Boston and Logan Airport. The toll collectors were close enough to yell updates about the family ("Lucy had a girl! Husband's still a drunk!"). Auntie Ida was the last to go. She got hit by a car walking home from the Walgreens on Porter Street. She was 93.

Lucille's brother, Anthony, looked like Wayne Newton, and not unintentionally. He wore a flagrant toupee that Phil only dreamed he could pull off. His chest hair curled over the thick gold chain nestled therein. A born Vegas guy. Phil and Anthony hit it off like crazy, as one might imagine.

After Lucy and Phil divorced, my dad was on his own again.

Either war or a woman had cared for him and carried him his whole life, and he wasn't particularly good at caring for himself. Only into our adult years did Lindsay and I see him go through long periods of bachelordom and feel his helplessness turned our way.

The house towered in the dark. I went down the short staircase with Henball. She wanted to see what ol' Guido Sarducci was up to.

The inner door was thin, and you could hear right through it. I heard my father yelling, distinct from the roar of the Patriots fans on the TV. His cry seemed pained, incommensurate with the simple stakes of enjoying a football game.

I knew there was no peace on the other side of the door. His yell had nothing to do with the simple accumulation of downs or yards or points but the monetary value assigned to each.

My father gambled. He breathed, he lied, he gambled, and then all the rest that makes up a life. Each decision and small act was imbued with hope. His risk-reward center weighed odds too favorably. When his hopeful wager was a loser, he looked betrayed by himself. He believed he'd win with his whole heart. And what is a gambling man but a dumb romantic who thinks things can change? He embodied the bettor's spirit.

I knew the names of the NFL teams before I knew the names of the states. Weekend visits with Phil often included Sundays in our hotel room with the game on, or in the lobby, or a sports bar, or a fast and friendly restaurant with TVs in the corners. He would ask me, phone dangling between ear and shoulder, "Who do you like? The Dolphins or the Steelers?"

I obviously preferred the Dolphins; I didn't know who or

what the Steelers were. I remember the feeling when the Dolphins lost, when we lost. It happened a lot, the hopeful start that ended in an L. It was always like that. There was a weight to knowing this in elementary school. It made me an adult instead of a child. And what kind of adult? The kind whose ears burned when too much was on the line. The kind who registered losses first and made decisions second. The careful kind, or put another way, the anxious kind.

I stood outside the door, wary. Henball asked if I was high or what. She knew better than I what ruin waited on the other side of that door. She had walked through doors like this since before I was born. In high-heeled alligator boots, no less.

The ruin, for her, was what? I wondered. A soothing constant? A turn-on? A habit? I could not understand my family. I have never understood my family.

I turned the knob and saw my father on his knees, on the carpet, inches from the television. His hands were on his bald head. He was shouting. He didn't see us for several seconds. My aunt and I stood inside the door, opened into a tragedy in action. My aunt, accustomed, pushed past me into the living room.

The carpet started a few feet inside the doorway, and concrete ran the perimeter of the room. The ceiling tiles were low and stained. Missing tiles gaped like missing teeth.

He didn't have my money. I knew it without stepping inside the apartment. I saw the exposed pipes, and I knew he didn't have my money. We were both on our knees in that moment, even though I stood above him.

I didn't hear him say this was the biggest upset in the history of upsets. No one saw it coming. You had to believe him. This was not supposed to happen.

The TV roared his disbelief back at us. His devastation was manifold and coming through in stereo. My aunt dropped onto the couch and kicked her pointy boots up on his chipped coffee table.

"What's goin' on, Phillipo Treskalini? Same ol', same ol'? What do you got to drink around here?"

She craned her neck around the apartment in the over-pronounced way of someone who wanted you to know they were looking and laughed in the hard way city girls were taught to laugh, teeth bared. To laugh with a blade in your bite was to laugh and do damage at the same time.

My aunt had taken my father's shit for a very long time, and now she smiled at his pained expression, that pathetic look on his face. Is there a scale that tracks disappointment into despair into rage? How many notes are on it? Half notes? How many runs up and down can a person take before they're off the charts?

Henball'd seen it. Oh, she'd seen it. She saw Phil's sad-eye routine when my mom kicked him out the first time, then again when we left Phil for good. Henball saw those sad eyes and knew they came out only when Phil was fucked. So she sat on his couch with her feet propped up and wanted a drink. No backstory, no bullshit. Just a drink.

But I believed him when he told me he was an old man now. That he'd given up gambling. I gave him my two hundred dollars because I was his kid. I was proud of that money, and I gave it to him with pride because I thought he'd give it back.

I wished I were as cool as my auntie on the couch, looking for a beer and nothing else. Knowing the score. Entirely un-shocked. My aunt was no idiot. She knew who we were dealing with here. Phil fell into his recliner. He put his head firmly in his hand. "I can't do this right now. I need to figure out what to do here. I need to get straight. I can't have my kid see me like this."

I loved my father. How do you love a man who'd been a monster without breaking or becoming one yourself? How do you become a woman immune, feet kicked up on the coffee table while men fell into ruin around you? These were the questions I asked my whole life because they were *the* questions of my whole life: to love them or not to love them? And which caused more despair? Were monsters really monsters, or were they merely the products and victims of monsters too? And what of those monsters? Who made them? Does that absolve? Can anything?

I wrote every crime in pencil.

He looked at me for the first time and said, "Nicole. Your dad fucked up royally. Let me take care of this, okay, and I'll see you tomorrow? Auntie will bring you back. This is my fault, but I'll fix it. Okay, Kiddo? I'll fix it, I swear."

Sweah.

The game clock ticked down on the TV and cemented a loss bigger than I understood. How bad was it? How much had he lost?

The truth was he wasn't only making bets. He was still taking bets and running books. He had lost so big he couldn't pay out the winnings. He would have to lay low. I had believed he would send me, his firstborn child, abroad made whole. No matter what else he put on the line, he wouldn't wager his child's security on a Patriots game. But what if he'd wagered his life?

How had I been so wrong about so much?

I spent the next few weeks bouncing around East Boston and Somerville, Winthrop and Revere, and I didn't hear from my dad. I sat in smoke-soaked pubs with my uncles, my mother's brothers, who said to me, "Listen: a thief is a thief is a thief." And they would know.

•

PHIL SLID FARTHER AND FARTHER down the couch until he was supine, his bad knee propped up on throw pillows. Before I realized it, he snored a gentle snore. I got him a blanket and covered him except his feet, clad in white athletic socks. He slept on his back with his limbs splayed, same as me. I took off his hat and his glasses and put them on the coffee table. As I walked into my bedroom, he mumbled deep from inside his drug slumber, "Hey, I think people can change. I think I changed. I can't believe I ate three of those fucking brownies."

Three brownies. He ate three of those fucking brownies. Phil lied first, then slowly revealed the truth. He was either too good at truth or too bad at lying. Perhaps both. Every day of his life, or mine at least. Calling my father a liar was not a charge that insulted him.

"I know. What do you want me to do about it?"

Or, once, unforgettably, "What? What's wrong with lying? I like it."

His responses were as infuriating as they were true. His honesty about lying might've been more refreshing if he weren't my father—if I hadn't always loved him, believed him and the things he said he'd do, his promises of next time. Could people change?

Did they need to change to be loved?

SOME KIND OF VICTORY

Phil and me, Harlem, November 2016

Phil woke from an anxious dream and called out to me. My dad dreamed about our dead family all the time, his visions aided by prescription drugs. I was asleep in my bedroom and opened my eyes to the framed poster of the 1986 Venice Carnivale that hung on the wall between my father and me. A pyramid of acrobats stood on one another's shoulders. I imagined they were family. Acrobat crews are always families—dependent, stacked on top of one another. Perhaps this was an overidentification with the strange people who set up and broke down their lives every day, then hauled off and did it again.

I got up and went into the living room. It was dark outside; it must have been the middle of the night.

"Oh, Nicole, sometimes I feel like it's closing in. Like my parents, my history, my inheritance, I mean my blood. This is my legacy. Get me my bag of pills on the desk in my room, will you?" My dad was awake and sober now. No matter where he was, my dad's desk was always loaded with active, expired, daily, and emergency pills. I looked at them and thought, *Those will be my legacy*. It was almost the holidays again, and the beginnings of that holy sadness moved through those early winter days and nights.

"I was holding Loretta, and she was in a dress with her shoulders out. I was saying, 'Loretta, the water is dirty. Get your feet out of the water. Get your feet out of the dirty water.' She was so beautiful, Nicole. You'd never believe it."

I sat with my dad on the couch, and we went back and forth about Auntie. Once he resurrected her in dreams and wanted to keep her alive when he was awake. But he didn't want to talk about the bad stuff. There was too much of it, and the dream had been enough. He wanted to talk about the holidays, the day trips, the Thanksgivings in Salem, the weekends in Marlborough.

He continued. "I woke up from this dream, this vivid dream of Dennis, dead, and Loretta, dead. I wonder if I'm not coming to my end."

Phil was manic. I could tell when he was revving—talking too fast, not listening, not unwinding.

"Why are they haunting me?"

I knew my father better than anyone else. His desires and fears were clear and pronounced on his face, in his voice. My father lied like he breathed, and yet he said himself true with every word. He was hard not to love, Phil. He was also hard to love. Phil the contradiction.

"Sometimes it's good to dream about the people you lose. To see them again," I said to my father. "You said the other day you're still in Vietnam. You told me yourself you'll never leave. I guess you're always in Somerville too, with Dennis."

Maybe most days he forgot. Maybe it was only some days he remembered that some part of him, of us, was still in that funeral home.

"Have you taken your meds today?"

Phil took three Xanax a day and had since 2000. When the doctor prescribed them, he said to my dad, "You'll never be off these again unless you want your heart to explode."

Three Xanax a day is a lot of Xanax, and Phil needed every one of them.

"I haven't. I took half a one this morning, but I didn't take the rest."

My father was dating Lourdes in St. Pete's, a younger Puerto Rican woman who took care of him, loved him, and drove him crazy. I knew after he spent time with Lourdes that he didn't feel that he needed his Xanax. But then, without it, the war of his life and the many battles within it came to collect, and my father spiraled. Sometimes I got confused as to why he couldn't live in the present. But then I thought about myself and my own anxieties, and I understood.

"I need you to eat something and take your pills and have a brandy and go back to sleep, okay?"

I brought him his gallon bag of pills and watched him rifle. The couch was wide enough for his shoulders and long enough that his feet didn't drop off it, a comfortable bed for an old man used to uncomfortable beds. I was glad he was here having his bad dreams with me. I refilled his E&J. He loved the cheap stuff.

"Why? You worried about the old man?" he asked. There was a thrill undeniable when women worried about Phil Treska. A clear light that shone out in smile and tone. He lived for it. Phil lacked guile. So did I. We are both idiots at subterfuge.

"Yes, of course I am. But mostly I want you relaxed. I'm trying to keep the old man around, you know?"

"That's a sweet kid. The best kid. I love your sister, but she doesn't take care of me. She doesn't understand me."

I didn't know if Lindsay avoided Phil's calls and questions because they scared her, or she couldn't be bothered, or because our dad went to prison when we were so small and she forgot who he was. But it was factual to say she didn't understand my father the way I did, and so he was mine to defend and tend to. For my life to proceed, for my world to keep turning, I needed him alive. And I knew—I *knew*—that wouldn't last forever.

I tried to turn the moment back to a place we could stay. A place that was pleasant.

"I think if you look at it right, it's kind of a nice dream. You got to see Loretta and Dennis again. Maybe it's a kindness."

Phil went quiet, then said, "Yeah, but he looked exactly the same as the day we buried him. The same shirt. I always remember his delicate hands were even more delicate when he was dead. And that's what I saw in my sleep. And that's what felt like a nightmare."

Whenever Phil and I got together, we drank wine and cried over everything: his sick sister, my sick auntie, and the anguish. His time in the war, and the anguish. The mob and its ways, which were not glamorous. I asked questions into the blurry night and filled up notebooks of quotes and names I'd heard before and I'd hear again. He answered my questions the way he always did—incomplete, the way he wanted to tell it. And I took my notes the way I always did—incomplete, catching the bits I wanted to know.

"That sounds terrible, Pops."

"Yeah," he said. "Had it been a conversation, or we were reuniting, that would've been different. But it wasn't like that. I'm glad I'm here to talk about it with you."

"I'm glad too."

"Maybe we can talk about it while I'm here. If that's okay. I know you carry it all."

I wanted to carry it all because if I didn't, I'd lose sight of it. And anyone will tell you, if you take your eye off the ball, it bounces. It breaks.

"Of course we can talk about it," I said.

I didn't say, *Who are you? And who am I?*

I wanted to climb the peaks of our lives and deaths and explore what they were made of before they melted back into earth.

What I didn't say was: *Please give me everything before you're gone.*

MY DAD LEFT DENVER WHEN he knew Lindsay was leaving Frank for good and selling the house. He'd stayed with her almost a year. Lindsay's job at the post office led her to an opportunity in the fire department. She fought for and won a position in the fire academy, with trainees ten and fifteen years her junior. She was starting over.

Phil wanted to start over too. He bounced between Vegas and Tampa, and then to Treasure Island, off St. Pete's Beach. He moved from flashy hotel room to brightly colored motel room up and down the strip, staying in places with signs that advertised rates by the week and the month. He rented for weeks at a time, gambling (oh, Phil, ever gambling) that the room would still be available when the clock ran out. Re-upping his housing little by little. Filling up his apartment tank, one gallon at a time.

Treasure Island was a kind of Wonderland for the retired East Coasters who lived on or near the strip of motels that lined the Gulf. Giant signs for the Thunderbird and the Don CeSar were visible for miles. At night, they lit up the ocean, the pink and turquoise and teal motels, the giant, perfect palms. No wonder Phil wanted to stay. It felt like escape, a way to sit near something immense and permanent. Treasure Island had everything: dancing and early bird specials and women you could peel off the floor at Sea Hags Bar and Grill at the end of the night. Go ahead, ask my dad. He'll tell you.

Phil told me he struck up a friendship with the woman who cleaned his favorite temporary apartment.

"Oh, yeah, she's your friend?" I said, suspicious.

"What! Only friends!" He swore to God. "She's married! What?"

Her family owned the building he was staying in and several more in the area. Phil chatted her up and down the hallway as she moved in and out of units. He was never more comfortable than when he was spending time with those doing the grunt work. He found them everywhere he went, the toilers. He treated them like gods and confidants, whether they liked it or not.

Turned out this lady was in a position to help him. She found him an apartment in one of her buildings off Treasure Island. She gave him a lease and a home at a price that allowed him to save a little money every month if he didn't make any bets. He signed the lease the day before he got on the plane for New York, and it was happy birthday, Phil.

I looked at my dad. How did he do it? How did he get these kind women to tend to him and care for him his whole life? Was it magic? Was Phil an angel too? Are angels real? Is my father a god in shambles at the door? Is he the one he taught us to look for? My father, who art in the basement, hallowed be thy name?

What did I know? What did I care? I was grateful we both had a home. I knew Phil was getting old, and it was getting harder for him to keep up with his bad habits on VA benefits and social security alone. I knew heart problems and stents had rattled his cage. So I was happy he'd found a place with a pool where he could watch the ocean change and read the paper. Old-man shit.

PHIL DRANK THE BRANDY I poured for his nerves. His eyes glazed over. He named his dead and some of mine. I told him: Go! Go make new friends in Florida! Phil said he didn't need friends anymore. No one he knew was alive anymore. Except me and Lindsay, and we were all he needed. That's a lot to be for someone, I said, their everything.

He put his brandy down on the coffee table, said he felt better.

I got up and moved the pile of legal documents and coffee-stained leases out of his way and put them in a drawer for the first time in months. The following year, the *Altman* case would be decided for the landlords. My lawyer at the time was a real proper guy, so when he told me I didn't stand a chance in hell, I believed him. I moved out in the summer of 2018. The landlords agreed to return my full deposit and drop the over

$8,000 in arrears I owed when I surrendered the apartment. I'd lost, but I walked away on my terms, clean. And it felt good. It felt like breaking even. And that, after years of fighting, felt like some kind of victory.

The Turk had taught me that fighting the good fight was what mattered, not winning. In fact, he said, losing was to be expected. It was a bad world. But you fought because it was the right thing to do, and you celebrated your victories, however small they seemed. They were important. And sweet.

This made sense to me. I spent my whole life fighting to not always be fighting and yet there I was—a love thug. I stood with my hands on my hips and said, *Listen up.* I told strangers, *Beat it*, and ran my mouth. And I never let go. I held on to everything I had for dear life. I picked fights on the streets. I always picked fight.

What I loved most about the Turk was what he taught me about myself. What I knew to be true, but hadn't named yet. I missed him, and I was angry he hurt me, but I couldn't hate him. He showed me outer space.

Phil said the pool at the new place was clean, and it was easy to find a private corner even if he had to listen to the other old-timers' right-wing talk radio bullshit. He loved working out alone in the early mornings. The gym was a treadmill and a set of weights and a small TV in a carpeted room that doubled as the building's community space. There was a bookshelf full of donated and well-worn romance and airport thrillers, travel guides and self-help books. He said he couldn't wait to add my book to the shelf one day.

It felt like victory, too, to talk to my dad about his new home without worrying about mine or Lindsay's. It was nice to know we were safe, for now. And it was nice having him on the couch, more drunk than stoned, getting sleepy and asking if people changed.

We talked about Lindsay and the kids in their new place. Lindsay found a townhome near the fire department and JJ's school. She decorated it with signs that read *Welcome Home* and *Kiss the Cook*. She inherited her neighbors' near-new bedroom sets and scoured Ross and Savers and her neighborhood bulletin board for couches, a smaller kitchen table, a vanity.

Phil told me about his apartment. He said that from his living room, you could see all the way to Tampa. Just follow the long line of palm trees tilting with the wind. And I told him it sounded very nice. I couldn't wait to see it, his home. And I meant it. We planned to spend a weekend at the pool when it got cold in New York.

"Forget the cold, Kid," he said. "Tell me something nice you remember."

SOMETHING NICE

Lindsay and Auntie Loretta at Dunkin' Donuts, Saugus, 2008

The last time I saw Auntie Loretta was in late 2008. It was also the last time Lindsay, Phil, and I were together in Boston. Phil lived in Newton then, with a new girlfriend and her two adult daughters, both pill addicts with open Child Protective Services cases. Lindsay was pregnant with Malia, the family's first new baby in a very long time, and I was saving money again, this time to move to New York.

We stopped at Regina's Pizzeria, the original location in the North End, and, over a meatball pizza with crushed red pepper, Phil told us that Elizabeth Warren lived next door to him.

"Great legs on her, the senator!" he said, and then, "I tell you what, I wouldn't kick her out of bed!"

Lindsay and I drank our root beers and shrieked, *Dad!* the same way we did when he said of our friends, "What? She's not my daughter!"

After dinner, we headed for the Sumner Tunnel out of Boston. When we were kids, we used to try to hold our breath the whole way under Boston Harbor, an impossible task. But not for Phil. He would hold his breath through miles of fluorescent lights, miles of white-knuckling it. He drove with his cheeks puffed out, or his arms flailing in overpronounced suffering. I thought he was a hero. Unstoppable. A god who didn't require oxygen—until I noticed he wasn't really holding his breath. I saw him breathe through his nose; I watched his chest rise and fall, and I didn't know what to feel. I never told Lindsay.

The three of us hit East Boston and followed the coast north past the rotaries and storage tanks and gravel yards until Revere Beach stretched out in front of us. A few people strolled the sidewalk or sat watching the water. The summer homes and condos were shuttered for the winter. Summer wasn't far behind us, but the shoreline felt preserved already.

We drove past Kelly's, past the professor's apartment on the point and the old Mickey Mouse cocktail lounge. We passed Papa's favorite house at the end of the beach, and took a left on Revere Street. We were headed for Route 1, that swift-running river flowing in and out of Boston.

But first, we passed the Showcase Cinema, an iceberg of a theater where Grammy Duca and I used to have the whole matinees to ourselves. We always left through the emergency doors on either side of the screen and found ourselves in a shock of sunshine.

My dad merged onto Route 1 North and pulled into Kappy's Fine Wine and Spirits for his evening nips. Up the road was Kowloon Chinese restaurant, a giant monument to tiki excess. The experience of Kowloon as a child was pure wonder and a little fear. Elaborate rooms unfurled in every direction into bars and stages and stairs and, somehow, bodies of water and palm trees. Getting lost and maybe even drowning were risks worth taking for the thrill of Kowloon's sweet and sour sauce.

Around the bend, the famed orange *Tyrannosaurus rex* lorded over the Route 1 Miniature Golf and Batting Cages. We went there every summer; they had the soft-serve ice cream I loved best, growing up. The mini golf closed in 2016, but the dinosaur, our beloved *Saugusaurus*, remained. A relic.

Farther up the road, a sixty-foot neon cactus sign announced the Hilltop Steak House, which closed in 2013. Its herd of fiberglass faux cattle, shellacked black and white, used to keep us company while we waited in long lines to be shuttled into three floors of steak tip specials, old-timey paper place mats, and gruff waitresses in checkered skirts.

They let me use the staff bathroom at the Hilltop once, when I was ten and got sick from too much A.1. sauce. I doused everything in sauce and syrup. I'm pretty sure I threw up in all of those restaurants along Route 1, at one point or another. I got sick when we stayed in hotel rooms. I got sick when we ate value meals and all-you-can-eat buffets.

And I got sick when it was time to go home; sick over how my dad got sick over it, how emotional he became when it was time to go. My family in Boston felt so demanding and intense, so foreign, and so utterly mine. I put the sauce to my mouth over and over to get to the part where I could let it all out.

And those brash servers in the dining room? Fifty years old in their gingham and frilly aprons? They cooed and comforted me, "Oh, honey, don't worry," in smoky Boston accents. They crowded around me and patted my back.

That run of road sparkled like Wonderland. The Golden Banana strip club, with its yellow-lettered eroding sign declaring it *World Famous*. Prince Pizza, its Leaning Tower of Pizza projecting off the roof at a jaunty angle. Their spaghetti was so oily. After that the highway tapered into the more mundane: chain motels, dealerships, and shopping malls.

Route 1's stops and signage managed to conjure a world bigger than the one we knew—the Far East, the Wild West, prehistory, Europe. Those holy restaurants off the highway promised us the big lights and far-flung places we might not otherwise see. There is some insistence of Bostonians, across generations, to live a life grand enough for the grandeur they feel. Even if there isn't much in their lives to indicate they should feel that way. My parents thought they were destined for greatness, even though greatness was not readily available to them. I liked to think that this was why they went after life so audaciously. I liked to think I inherited this from them. The *audacity*.

And like Wonderland, we flocked to Route 1 until we didn't. That Kowloon still existed—that Kelly's and Mike's and Regina's and Kappy's and Sabella's and Jeveli's still existed—I suppose that's why we revered them so much. They were there, ours. Our Boston was a Boston that got sliced and diced to the point that it was a wonder anything could stay. Of course we revered some kind of permanence—something to point to and say, "I came from right here." The Cyclone roller coaster on Revere Beach burned in 1969, and they didn't tear it down until 1974. There was yearning in what remained.

My whole life I'd thought that we were different, my mom and us kids. That our ten homes on Oahu and my six first grades made us strange from our family. But that wasn't so true. We came from people who got kicked out of every home they'd ever known, their houses torn down to make way for a better day that never came. For progress. We knew home was what we made it. Irrespective of where we settled, everything changed.

Everything changed.

Everything changed even as much of life remained the same.

Across Boston, the signifiers of home were disappearing. Well, my home, at least. Somerville wasn't Slumerville anymore, and Eastie had glassy high-rises and well-maintained bike paths full of women with perfect ponytails. My family was moving out or dying, and people were moving across the harbor *on purpose.* Boar's Head was no longer an elite cold cut. They sold it everywhere. The Hilltop was gone, the mini golf was gone, but the signs remained. The *Saugusaurus* still teetered, his giant eyes rolled skyward. *Buddy, don't I know it.* There was longing in those ruins, I tell you.

And you know what? I was glad for all the glowing ghosts around Boston, reminding me of the home that once belonged to us.

I looked backward too. At our city, our family, our bodies getting dragged through time. I was the same as my mother and father. The anxiety and insecurity and townie fear was still there. I turned on the accent, the movements, the phrases. All of it. I could wear it, when I wanted, like an oversized Red Sox sweatshirt.

And I did to my stories what my parents did to their stories. I used them as a shield, a validation, a comfort. I was my mother and my father; my aunties and uncles; the sad ones, the monstrous ones, the MTA and New England Bell and Post Office and Boston Police ones. I was the crazy sister who never left home, the sad brother who couldn't make it on his own. I'd leave, over and over, but I couldn't get outside of us, spinning the myths we need to spin to escape feeling caught in a big, gray trap. But at least I got out. A victory over gravity on my mother's part. A rending of the universe.

I was doing the same thing my parents did, writing a Boston that existed in my memories and recollections, in yellow-edged pictures of cousins and uncles and aunts dead of heroin, tumors, alcohol, and mental illness. I was writing a Boston that was gone. And yet it was the place I always returned to, shocked at how innate it felt, how in my bones the place was.

I'd accomplished the great trick of escape, like Houdini on the Charles, only to realize I carried Boston with me wherever I went. And what a fool to even wonder.

My mother packed our homes into houses, and then back again. She drove anywhere from two to four kids across the country, while my stepdad deployed to Europe and Asia for years. Ever a Bostonian, she built beauty over the swamp of things, over and over, and taught us to do the same.

Each monument off Route 1 was holy to me. Each stop at Kappy's, waiting under the red blinking sign while my dad ran inside? *Church and holy water, Kid.* I've been in the Hilltop's private spaces, and the high priestesses there took care of me. It was my city too. And according to Ha-Ha, my saying so said so. If ever I doubted myself, my belonging, all I had to do was look at my whole life laid out in flashing lights. *Don't forget,* they blinked, *where you come from.*

My grammy used to send care boxes after we moved away to make sure we remembered. Cold cuts, provolone, ravioli. Everything wrapped in butcher paper and shipped in dry ice. She used the delivery method hospitals used to transport organs. Pecorino, capicola, bresaola arrived in heavily insulated boxes marked FRAGILE, THIS SIDE UP. Scali bread, pepperoni, and sweet sausage: heavy, essential, sliced paper-thin.

I thought I wanted distance between myself and where I'd come from. But that wasn't true. I felt overwhelmed with gratitude that we had existed there, at all.

I was no different from my parents.

WE ARRIVED AT AUNTIE LORETTA'S before dark. The home looked grand from the outside. It didn't look like the other places where my auntie had lived. It looked nice. Wide porches and Adirondack-style chairs dotted the manicured lawn. We parked near a maple at the height of its autumnal glory, shaking its gold leaves in the New England dusk.

In the lobby, there were soft couches and a fireplace. The coffee tables were sprayed with glossy brochures. When we passed through the arched doors into the interior, the place stopped feeling so stately and started to feel more like a hospital. Fluorescent light bounced off white tile. The lighting and the smell were antiseptic. Even though there were plants and paintings, the place felt underwater, overlit. Impossible, like the Sumner Tunnel.

"Girls, welcome to Oz," Phil said. He waved to the nurse at reception. She shouted, "Happy belated, Phil! Loretta's been telling everyone."

"Thanks, Joan. Not bad for an old guy, huh?" Phil struck a strongman pose, and Lindsay and I rolled our eyes. We waved at Joan, as if to say, *Get a load of this guy. What can you do?*

But Joan loved it. She *Oh, Phil*'d him with a playful swat and led us past the desk and into the residential wing. Once she went back to her station, Phil whispered, "Here come the munchkins. Watch. They've been waiting for us."

And sure enough, down the long hallway lined with single rooms, my auntie's neighbors emerged, each in their own states of grace and disorder. They left behind blaring televisions and half-eaten sandwiches from the cafeteria to see what there was to see.

The neighbors smiled and hugged us. They smoothed Lindsay's and my curls and told us we were young and beautiful. They asked us when we'd be back and why we hadn't met before. They were fantastic company. Then they led us to Loretta in the courtyard, lit by floodlights.

"She's always out here," one of the women told me. "Always, always, always. Even when we have something special. We don't get that many visitors, can you believe that?" She was a born gossip. I loved her.

I followed my dad through the glass door. Loretta sat in profile, very straight and clutching her pocketbook. She had on slacks with a lavender blouse—and no jacket in the cold. She smoked and ran her hand over the short hairs at the back of her neck. Her hair was thin and copper red. I wondered who dyed it and combed it, who remembered to rinse well.

My auntie wore hot pink lipstick, the same as when I was a kid. She was dressed up and waiting for us. When she stood, her purse fell on the floor.

"Oh my god, Nicole, you look just like Ma. Like a photograph," she said, and then she touched Lindsay's pregnant stomach. "That's how it works, isn't it?" Her laughter exploded, and she hugged her girls.

"You still know me. Don't you? You remember me. I can tell."

Phil came over and said, "All right, Loretta, that's enough for now. They just got here. Let's show the girls your place and get your coat. Aren't you cold? Are you ready for a night out on the town?"

Phil bought her a winter coat at Burlington, the previous October. Loretta told us her friends at the home were jealous so she only wore it when it was really cold. Phil told her that was the craziest thing he'd ever heard.

"Well, what do you think we're doing here, Philip?"

My dad held the door open for his family and watched his sister herd his daughters past her lingering neighbors and into her room. She didn't want to share.

Her room was small and concrete with control panels by the door and next to the bed. It was like a bunker or a glorified hospital room. Her dresser and bed took up half the space and they weren't even hers; they were the home's. A loaner life, that was what my auntie lived. There was a couch from one of the sitting rooms, a television against one wall, and a sink and small refrigerator against the other. No stove. The television and dresser were piled with pills and pictures, just like at my dad's.

There was toddler me sitting on Auntie's knee, laughing in the backyard at Hancock Street; Phil in Vietnam at nineteen, blurry with a gun. Lindsay picked up his picture and tried to decipher the look on his face. I found my third-grade picture on the wall. My front teeth were missing. The little girl looked out at herself without recognition, still a child, still her aunt's companion.

My auntie lived with ghosts, I thought. She surrounded herself with the relics and ruins of what pointed the way home, even though home was long gone. My auntie's holy little room, full of its shrines and sacred objects, brought her comfort and brought her back to herself, to us.

In the bathroom, her Wet n Wild lipstick was on the sink with a can of Aqua Net and a collection of medications. Just like at Hancock Street. And what was a life, really, but a collection of cosmetics, old pictures, and little plastic bottles? We carried what we could, and Loretta couldn't carry much. Each item in her little room was a totem, blessed by its mere existence, its survival.

"Nicole, you okay in there? Come on, we're going to Dunkin' Donuts."

"Gimme a minute!"

I washed my face with cold water, and my eyes were mostly clear when I opened the door. My auntie had her quilted winter coat on and showed it off to my sister, spinning around with her arms out. Lindsay applauded, and Auntie said, "Oh, honey. Let's go get a cruller. They're my favorite."

At the Dunkin' Donuts in Saugus, a teenager in a purple polo with coffee stains took our order. Another pushed a mop around the empty room, its yarn head slopping back and forth and getting caught on the legs of the plastic furniture. We were the only customers, and we took a table by the window with our French crullers and decafs.

Loretta sang us her favorite Dean Martin song, "Non Dimenticar," a song we'd known all our lives. Her voice filled the room, slow and sad. Don't forget, she sang, that when love comes it's celestial. And don't forget that when it leaves, we wait alone and dream of its return. For lifetimes, sometimes, we wait for love's light to shine on us again. We hope not to be forgotten.

Non dimenticar.
Non dimenticar.
Don't forget, my darlings.

Phil watched her sing and smiled, wiping crumbs off the table. The orange lights from the Dunkin' Donuts sign lit the night and held us in its warm glow. The teenagers behind the counter stopped to watch the woman with the rusted, untuned voice. It wasn't because she was loud or crazy. They worked a half mile from a mental home; we were nothing new. They listened to my auntie because she sang of grief and love like everyone should know it.

ACKNOWLEDGMENTS

Thank you to my dear friend and agent, Annie DeWitt, for your love and support. And to the magnificent Leslie Shipman for taking a chance on me. I cannot thank my editor, Yahdon Israel, enough. Without you, this book would still be coiled in my mind. Thank you to cover designer Jackie Seow for an amazing cover, and to the incredible editorial team who made *Wonderland* a beautiful book. Thank you to Sasha Rudensky for the most perfect author photos.

Thank you to John J. Devine Jr., reference librarian at the Boston Public Library, for answering my many questions. Thank you to the *Boston Globe* archives for providing a relatively trustworthy time line of the Treska family. A tremendous thank-you to Stephen R. Wilk for *Lost Wonderland* and Edward and Frederick Nazzaro for *Revere Beach's Wonderland: The Mystic City by the Sea*, two books I referenced repeatedly.

Thank you to my forever first reader and best girl, Catherine Foulkrod. And to Tracy O'Neill for spending years pacing and sweating and laughing with me. Writing our books together was a dream. And to the rest of our Open City dream team—Kimberly King Parsons, Robb Todd, Diana Marie Delgado, Caleb Gayle, and Joe Riippi. A special thank-you goes out to my most brilliant Carrie Cooperider, and our fearless leader, Mitchell Jackson.

ACKNOWLEDGMENTS

Thank you to my greatest advocate and teacher, Gordon Lish. Thank you to Louise Glück for anointing this book. Thank you to Amy Hempel. Thank you to Linsey Abrams, Fred Reynolds, Yana Joseph, and Michelle Valladares at CCNY, and to all my teachers. Thank you to my students. I am forever grateful to you.

In memory of Giancarlo DiTrapano, a good shepherd. Thank you to Lia, LJ, Giu, and the Giancarlo DiTrapano Foundation for their friendship and generosity; and to Maria and Pierre for sharing their love, music, and magic with me. My time with you while working on *Wonderland* was a true gift. Thank you to the Jerome Foundation, for their early support.

Thank you to my dad, Phil, for writing this book with me. And to my mom, Christine, for saving me. To Lindsay, my soulmate. And to Chelsea and Michael, my babies, forever. To Malia and JJ, my darlings. The future is bright and has a dry sense of humor.

Thank you to Doris for the time, support, and editing skills. Thank you to Eugene, Julia, and the Rudenskys for taking me in. Same goes for Casey, Kelly, and Claudia Gordon. And John Sharkey, Mr. Sharkey, and also Mary Sharkey. I love you guys. To Alexi, Brittany, Kate, Anne, and David—my biggest cheerleaders. To Lisa, thank you for helping me keep my mind right. To the D-town crew, thank you for a lifetime of love. Thank you to Beyoncé, Lana, Ani, Tori, and Kate.

Finally, and most importantly, thank you to my husband, James. My love. My default editor. My best friend. And also to my dog, Nadine. Thank you for making sure I left the house on deadline.

ABOUT THE AUTHOR

NICOLE TRESKA lives in Harlem with her husband, James, and their three-legged dog, Nadine. *Wonderland* is her first book.